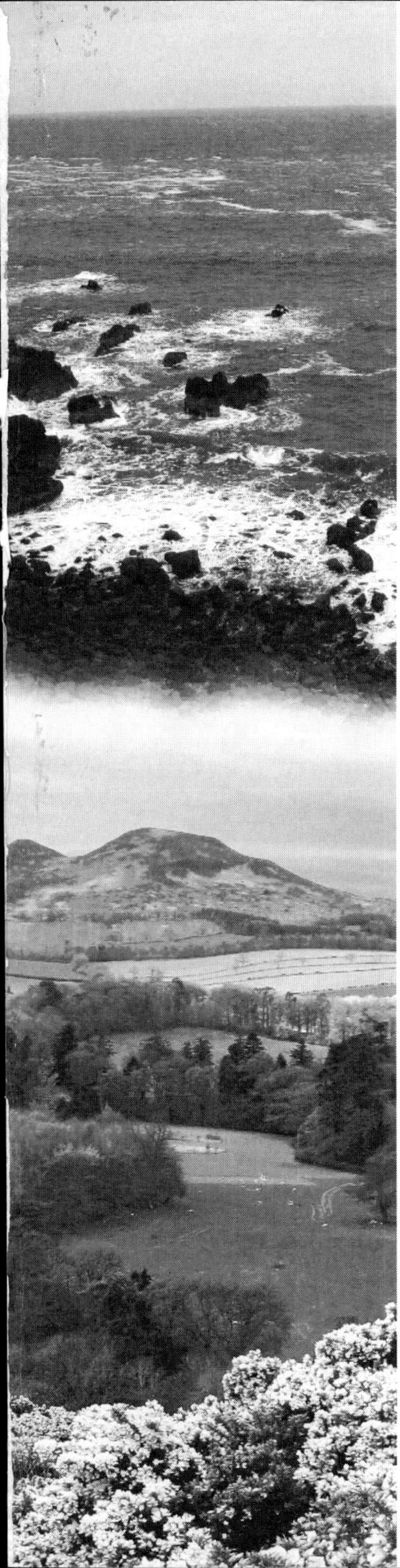

Border Voices

COAST & COUNTRYSIDE

An Anthology from
Borders Writers' Forum

Cover photographs:
St Abbs Head
Scott's View

This anthology is a taster of Borders Writers' Forum members' writing on the theme of "Coast & Countryside" in the Borders.

Further information on the Forum and its members can be found at: www.borderswritersforum.org.uk and on Facebook.

Borders Voices COAST & COUNTRYSIDE
An Anthology from Borders Writers' Forum

Copyright © Individual members of Borders Writers' Forum April 2019
Copyright © for photographs remains with individual members' submissions or Tony Parkinson.

All rights reserved
No part of this publication may be reproduced, stored in a retrieval system, or transmitted in any form or by any means, without the prior permission in writing of the publisher, nor be otherwise circulated in any form of binding or cover other than that in which it is published and without a similar condition including this condition being imposed on the subsequent purchaser.

British Library Cataloguing-in-Publication Data
A CIP catalogue record for this book is available from the British Library

ISBN: 978-0-9926261-7-4

Cover design: Sarah Thompson Text pages: Tony Parkinson

Published by:
Borders Writers' Forum
c/o Double Elephant Associates
Orchard Cottage, Lanton
Jedburgh, Scottish Borders TD8 6SX
www.borderswritersforum.org.uk

COAST & COUNTRYSIDE

Foreword

Welcome to the sixth anthology of Border Voices. Between these pages you will find local writers responding to the varied scenery of the Scottish Borders. Towns and villages, castles and historic houses, each with their own distinctive character, are set in over 1800 square miles of glorious countryside. Through it flows the River Tweed, fed by numerous tributaries on its journey to the North Sea at Berwick. It is a landscape shaped for centuries by humans and which in turn has shaped their history.

These voices take us, in poetry and prose, from Lindisfarne to riverside mills, from ancient tales to modern dilemmas. There is humour, history, fantasy and acute observation. Here you can be drawn into powerful myths; soar with a sea-eagle; immerse yourself in the distinctive character of spoken Scots; journey the length of the Tweed; learn about one of the Borders' lesser-known sons.

Borders Writers' Forum exists for writers at all stages of their writing careers, offering support and mutual encouragement. This book reflects the diversity of its members' styles and interests, through the prism of the coast and countryside of this wonderful, and often overlooked, part of Scotland.

Jane Pearn
Chair, Borders Writers' Forum

Border Voices
COAST & COUNTRYSIDE

Title	Author	Page
The Cowrie Shell	Anita John	5
Contemporary Settings - Historical Fiction	Margaret Skea	6
Fulmar	Robert Leach	12
The Gully	Robert Leach	13
Foxgloves	Robert Leach	14
On St Abbs Head	Iona Carroll	15
Countryside and Coast	Tom Murray	19
Tweed	Jane Pearn	20
You go for a walk	Jane Pearn	22
Mirror	Jane Pearn	24
The Borders Countryside	Raghu Shukla	25
Hold up the Fish	Keith Hall	29
The Gorse in Bloom	Pamela Gordon Hoad	30
Newhaven	Andrew James Paterson	36
The Swimming Lesson	Andrew James Paterson	37
A Lad o'Pairts	Rosalyn Anderson	39
The Journey	Laurna Robertson	46
Ripples	Sarah Johnston	48
The Long View/ Sea Eagle	Anne Stormont	53
Coming Home	Vee Freir	54
Troubled Waters	Barbara Pollock	56
Still runs the Teviot	Toni Parks	62
Welcome to the House of Fun	Sandra Craig	64
Unleashed	Hayley M. Emberey	67
Contributors		71

The Cowrie Shell
by Anita John

From silver and agate, citrine and amethyst,
bloodstone and freshwater pearls,
I choose the cowrie shell

that I might carry it
as the sea has carried it,
turning it over and over like finger and thumb

before bringing it finally to the water's edge.
Where someone has found it –
someone sifting through stones

and shells of many iridescent colours –
has found this gem, unseen at first,
as the grey plover might go unnoticed

until it takes flight,
the sun glinting silver from the underside of wings.
So too this *groatie buckie*.

Someone has washed away the sand,
to let the shades of milky white and rose
shine through like polished porcelain.

From silver and agate, citrine and amethyst,
bloodstone and freshwater pearls,
I choose the cowrie shell

scarcely bigger than my pinkie
but a powerful charm –
bringer of luck, protector from harm,

worn close to my heart
it will bring forth, with ease, my children.
May they carry it too

as I will carry it,
turning it over and over in finger and thumb
to pass to my children, to their daughters and sons.

Groatie buckie: Orkney dialect for cowrie shell.

Contemporary Settings - Historical Fiction
by Margaret Skea

Five historical novels and several awards later, I still find it hard to believe, and even harder to say, 'I'm an author', when someone asks me what I 'do'.

But ask me about setting in fiction and I hope you have half-an-hour to spare, for giving the reader a 'you are there' experience ranks highly amongst my many writing passions and I'm never short of words on that topic. Not because it is easy for me. Quite the reverse.

My first (and best) advice to any fledgling writer is always, if at all possible, to visit the locations they want to use. Not too difficult if you're writing contemporary fiction, set within your own environs, or at least within easy reach, but rather more tricky, time-travel aside, when writing about historical characters in the west of Scotland in the 16th century, as I was in my first novel. Adding France and The Hague into the mix for the later books in the series compounded the problems. And, when I chose to begin a new series set in the Reformation period in Saxony, you could be forgiven for thinking I'm a glutton for punishment. However, this anthology focuses on the Borders' coast and countryside, so here I will concentrate on aspects of the local landscape that became vital tools to enable me to evoke the setting my 16th century Scottish characters inhabited.

But first, some background. The Munro series is rooted in the Ayrshire Vendetta, a notorious clan feud involving the Cunninghame and Montgomerie families in the south-west of Scotland. The county of Ayrshire still exists of course, but not the Ayrshire I needed to depict. Some features of landscape remain relatively untouched through the centuries – the hills haven't moved – though it appears from early maps and from my own knowledge of coastal geology that the coastline may have.

Early maps are beautiful, as any perusal of those drawn by Timothy Pont, and reproduced in Blaeu's 1654 Atlas of Scotland, shows. But, however impressive, they cannot be considered reliable by 21st century standards, except in the broadest of terms. The process of map-making was still very much a work-in-progress. Aside, however, from the issue of inaccuracy, modern-day Ayrshire is very different from that of the

16th century in many respects. As well as the possible alteration of the shoreline, towns and villages have sprung up inland to mask the original terrain, woods have been cut down, fields enclosed and marshes drained. Roads have cut across valleys, rivers have changed course, lochs have silted up and extensive mining activity has left its mark, so that it can be hard to picture in detail the Ayrshire of the 1580s and 90s.

Take, for example, the historic event known as the Massacre of Annock, with which I open my first novel, *Turn of the Tide*. It is well-documented, but it's no longer possible to establish the site of the ambush with any degree of certainty, though it's likely it's been swallowed up in modern Stewarton. When trying to choreograph the event all I had to go on were a couple of sentences from an 18th century source:

> '*the Cunninghams assembled to the number of thretie-four ... and concealed themselves in a low ground near the bridge of Annock ... all of a sudden the whole bloody gang set upon the earl and his small company ...*'

It's possible to examine the river outside of the town, but all that provides is a sense of the scale of it and even that may not reflect the situation in the 16th century. Several years ago, I was asked to meet up at Annock with some members of the Clan Cunningham Society of America. I knew they harboured hopes of seeing the actual massacre site, but the best I could promise was to walk a stretch of the river with them and hopefully provide a sense of what it might have been like to wait for the opposing clan to appear. In *A House Divided,* I send one of my key fictional characters into an existing cave complex. There is historical evidence both that the caves were used as hiding places for smuggled goods and that they were avoided by local people, who considered them to be haunted – likely a convenient fiction begun by the smugglers themselves. A perfect location then for a key character to use as a hiding place. However, the entrance to these caves is now inaccessible, set halfway up a cliff face. Clearly this wasn't the case in my period, indicating the extent to which a river can cut a gorge through the surrounding land. This in turn informed my depiction of other rivers and river courses involving gorges.

'Place' was an extremely important concept in 16th century Scotland and men were often referred to by the name of their home rather than their surname. This was helpful in terms of the story – avoiding the potential confusion of multiple characters with both the same Christian and surnames, of whom there are many – but it did increase the importance of location and the consequent difficulties of lack of physical evidence. Most of the relevant castles in Ayrshire no longer exist and their exact locations cannot be pinpointed. This was a very real problem for me, both practically and emotionally, as I tried to think my way into the heads of real people, without the clues that their own environment might have provided.

Take Braidstane, for example, where Kate Munro and her children live in *A House Divided*. From the *Montgomery Manuscripts,* I know that Braidstane was

'in the bailliary of Kyle in the county of Ayr',

but no trace of the tower remains. Admittedly that gives me leeway. For the sake of the story, Kate can live in a bastle house associated with the main tower, whether or not one actually existed there. I can conveniently imagine a gable window facing whatever direction I please, but, fiction writer or not, I'd happily have traded in those advantages for a glimpse of the real thing. There are some stumps of castles of the right scale, but there's a world of difference between standing within the crumbling remains of a tower house and imagining what it must have been like to live there.

Fortunately small-scale 16th century tower houses were little more varied in layout than those in the average modern housing scheme, usually conforming to one of several basic designs, the three most popular being rectangular, L-shaped, or Z-shaped. Plans are readily available – Nigel Tranter, aside from his prolific fiction output, also produced an illustrated five-volume series – *The Fortified House in Scotland*, which, happily, my local library had in stock. But the choice of decoration and evidence of the placing of amenities such as the kitchen range and garde-robes (the 16th century equivalent of en-suite) would have provided welcome insights into the individual tastes and preferences of my characters and have helped to transform them into living, breathing people.

In the absence of existing Ayrshire locations to describe, it made more sense for me to look at examples close to home and the tower houses in my novels are amalgams of the many I've visited, both ruined and complete, of those that litter the Borders countryside. There are three real towers that were particularly important to me. Greenknowe, which features on the cover of *A House Divided*, is a typical tower of my period, built in 1581 and is a ruin, though with most of its outer walls remaining. It provided the perfect exterior for the home of my fictional main family, especially as at the outset of the book their home too is a ruin.

Its near neighbour, Smailholm, is almost 100 years older and simple in form, but complete. Although unfurnished, I could count the stairs between each floor, time myself running up them and feel how out of breath I was by the time I reached the top. I could perch in a window reveal and see the ground stretching away below me and hear the wind howling down the chimney. It is set in a rugged, untouched and utterly atmospheric landscape and as it, like the others, is within easy reach of my home, I was able to visit it in all weathers. This was an important element in my research. While maps and, indeed, photographs can indicate terrain, there is nothing like walking the ground in sunshine, rain, wind and snow to ensure an accurate evocation of setting, whatever the season.

The third goes by the interesting name of Fatlips Castle, which, though semi-derelict at the time I was writing, nevertheless retained a beautifully decorated timber ceiling (similar to those in Gladstone's Land in Edinburgh). If you think that the current austerity of the exterior of Scottish tower houses was matched by dull interiors, think again.

This castle has now also been restored and can be visited by obtaining a key in the nearby village of Denholm.

It was easy to set scenes in royal palaces, such as Holyroodhouse and Stirling Castle, also now beautifully restored. However, the key characters' homes I designed, as I might a modern 'kit house', with elements chosen from all local options, in order to best satisfy the needs of both setting and story.

In *By Sword and Storm,* key characters travel by ship from The Hague to Edinburgh. Although the historical characters did make that journey, we have no documentary evidence of the exact timing, nor any details of the journey itself. However, from other research it is clear that in the 16th century they would have, as far as possible, hugged the coastline as they travelled northwards from the English Channel. The section of that coastline which I know best lies between north Northumberland and Edinburgh. Therefore, I chose to set most of the fictional key events of that journey between those two points.

All of this neatly illustrates the balance that I try to preserve: between historical fact and fiction, accuracy and authenticity and the important role that today's landscape plays in the creative decisions I have to make.

Fulmar
by Robert Leach

Arrow swooping down,
Looping away, yellow point
More bludgeon than rapier,
Eye black-cruel ...

We thought this beach our own,
Arriving from deserted roads carved
From tough-grass empty lands –
Straw-yellow beach, sky
Innocence-blue, and the sea
Plangent, puckered with wavelets.

You couldn't wait to bathe,
And not a soul nearby to spy
Your nudity – pink
In the sun's caress;
And your splashing – like a five-year-old
Trying on the world

Till the bullet fulmar
Came to claim his own –
Sorcerer spirit from the sky,
Maybe, or guardian for the gods
Of emptiness, preternity,
Space, place – the lost dream
Before the coming of the chaos of man.

The Gully
by Robert Leach

At first you think, All's still
In this lair of timelessness, this
Lost place, dry ditch, which once
Perhaps was a stream, now
A mere mnemonic
For seasons past.

Drifts of crisp leaves, broken, brown,
Lie stiff on bumps of earth or jutty roots;
A spike of bracken's trapped
In the dead fronds of years gone;
Trunks of trees
Are rigid as stopped clocks.

Then you hear sparrow or tom tit
Scrabble at the silence,
A whim of wind urging green leaves
To surge, fall back,
And surge again. Again
Time moves.

Foxgloves
by Robert Leach

After the belly-rumble of storm,
The river prancing and lurching,
(Whitewash whipped to a sprint),

And a lone gull
Flung like Monday's washing
Under the running sky –

A man, a mower,
Gold baseball cap back to front,
Face tight as an orange

In the mud-grey light,
Swishing with a scythe
At tufts and nettle shoots,

And the deft
Whispered odour
Of the foxgloves.

On St Abbs Head
by Iona Carroll

It was the woman who saw it first. She was unsure what it was and so she stopped walking, leaning on her hazel stick for support. There was a shape behind a rock on a grassy patch at the edge of the track. Most days she and Archie walked along this way. A second or two later, she resumed walking, talking to her husband in a hushed voice, but Archie, being slightly deaf now, didn't answer. He was already past the shape and away in his own world which he was more often than not these days.

'Archie,' she called, louder this time.

'Whit is it noo?' He turned to face his wife and said. 'Wull ye no daunder on wumman, thare's a storm comin.'

And sure enough, the black clouds were gathering over St Abbs Head and the air had turned cooler.

'Leuk, ower yonder… next tae yon muckle stane …'

'Cannae see ocht!'

'Ir ye blinn, man? Ower yonder!'

Archie took a step backwards and now he could see what was there, almost hidden behind the rock. He shook his head.

'Oo shuid gaun on. Dinnae fash yersel. Ye cannae dae ocht for it, Aggie.'

But the woman wasn't convinced. She leaned over the shape and prodded it.

'Oo maun dae summit… the puir wee burdie's bin hurtit.'

'Thrapple it. Yons whit I wad dae for it.'

Upon hearing his words, Aggie looked up and shook her stick, ever so slightly, but enough.

'Ye'll dae nae sic a thin, Archie MacDonald. The puir critter. Can ye no see, it's bracken a weeng.'

And sure enough, that was what she had first noticed; the white shape of a feather lying next to the rock, and the small bird unable to move. Thinking of her husband's words, Aggie sighed. She was a kind woman. The sight of the injured bird, the gentle black eye looking ever so fearful, the yellow beak open and hissing its vulnerability to the dangers it faced. Aggie, uncertain of what to do, felt her own heart beat faster for she hated to see another creature in pain. All her life she had cared for the unfortunate and less able and, if sometimes, those she looked after appeared ungrateful, this compassionate woman would forgive them, and in no time, she would find another creature, human or animal, to nurture. The bird made a feeble attempt to stand up on its spindly black legs but the effort was not enough and it sunk down again onto the grassy patch. Both Aggie and Archie could see the injury on the wing clearly now. Blood oozed from the damaged wing and some tiny red droplets had settled further down towards the small black triangle on the wing tip.

'It's a wee kittiwake... maun hiv bin skaithed somewey whan the ithers flew awa,' Archie said.

It was the end of summer and the sea birds had left the high cliffs. With their going, the tourists and the bird watchers would disperse and calm would return to the St Abbs area. But, come the spring, the birds would return to nest once again on the steep black cliffs, to lay their eggs, so precariously balanced upon the ledges, and the cliffs would once again resound to the screams and calls of guillemots, razorbills, kittiwakes and gulls as thousands of birds squabbled for nesting spaces. Then the tourists and walkers would return as well, and be amazed at the sight of so many different birds along the shore and the cliffs as puffins, shags and the beautiful yellow and white gannets swooping downwards, torpedo-like, into the sea, for St Abbs Head was a magic seabird city on the Berwickshire coast.

'Win awa noo Aggie. Thare's nowt oo can dae for the wee burdie. This yin wullnae be jynin it's neebors for the lang journey oot tae the sea.'

Their eyes met, and such a feeling of sadness passed between them at that moment. They had often talked about the migration of their sea birds from the cliffs of St Abbs. It was a fact, Aggie said, that the birds saw so much of the world and it was also a fact, that neither she nor Archie had ventured very far, albeit once across the border to Newcastle and a few times to Edinburgh. They had met each other at the Herring Queen Festival when Aggie was sixteen and Archie, who had grown up in Eyemouth, was seventeen. That had been the beginning of their life together. They were married a few years later at the Eyemouth Kirk. Archie had moved in with Aggie in St Abbs, for Aggie could not leave her poor father, bedridden most of the time with arthritis.

'Weel, aw the kittiwakes ir awa noo, cept this yin,' sighed Archie. 'Oo wullnae be seein thaim agane tul the spring, thaim aw feedin on the weeng an gan tae furrin airts oo'll nivver see.'

'Ay I ken.'

There was an air of finality about the statement, the certainty of life's transience. They were both nearing the end of their lives together.

'Oo'd better leave the wee burdie noo. Leuk at the sky, the wund's stertin tae blaw coorse... thare's stormy wather on the wey.'

A few drops of rain had already fallen and the feathers of the injured bird were sprinkled with moisture. The rain droplets had caused some of the blood on the bird's broken wing to trickle downwards onto the white feather.

They were about to move away when the kittiwake suddenly moved. It thrust its tiny body upwards, trembling, and for a poignant brief second it stood on frail little legs. The tip of the broken wing, now dangling and helpless, lay on the soft earth. The bird then let out an almighty squawk.

'Leuk, Archie, the wee burdie's leevin. Whit a fechter this wee yin is. Gin I wes to tak it hame wi iz...mebbe I cuid mend it's weeng... I've clooted up a wheen o puir wee critters in ma time, hiv I no juist?'

'That ye hiv, Aggie. That ye hiv.'

'I cuid leuk efter it for the wunter... an in the spring...?'

'Ay. Whan its sibs cam hame...?'

'Oo cuid gie it a wee shot, div ye no think?'

'Haud ma stick for iz, Aggie.'

With a sudden movement Archie knelt over the kittiwake, cradling the bird ever so gently in his large fisherman's hands. He ran his index finger downwards from the head of the bird to the tip of its tail, and all the while the captive bird hissed and trembled. It tried with one last valiant effort to bite the fingers of Archie's hand. He murmured softly as if saying a prayer, and then in a flash, it was all over.

'Och, Archie…'

Gently was that moment between life and death as Archie laid the dead kittiwake next to the rock where they had first noticed it, and this time he positioned the little bird so that the broken wing was on the ground and the good wing was visible.

'Ye cuidnae hiv saufed this yin, lass. It widnae hiv lested throu the nicht, whit wi the trashie rain an mebbie a tod oot leukin for its denner, the burd had nae hope.'

Archie took his stick from Aggie, and held her hand like they always did on their walks together, for both of them were less steady on their feet these days, and it was good to have each other.

'Pull yersel thegaither lass an haud yer wheesht! Oo'll mak oor wey hame for the tea. Oo dinnae want to be caucht in this haar, div oo noo?'

Aggie nodded. Her face, wet from the raindrops and the tears that ran down her cheeks, looked towards the mist covering the cliffs of St Abbs Head. There wasn't a seabird to be seen. She gave Archie's hand a familiar squeeze and the old couple turned to walk back along the track that they had walked together for so many years; this same track where once Aggie had skipped as a child, and in all weathers. She often thought that she knew every blade of grass, every pebble along the way, for was it not so that her whole life had been contained within these few miles? She imagined the young kittiwake and how it might have been for it on its first journey away from the cliffs that she, too, called home. How wonderful it would be to be able to soar upwards to the sky, and turn and fly down to the endless sea below, then duck and dive and feed on the wing and find your way, by some miraculous compass, to foreign shores so far, far away from the cliffs of St Abbs.

Archie's hand was firm in hers. He was a good man. Had always been a good man, and that was something after all.

'Ay, Archie,' she said to him when their cottage came into view, 'it wis for the best, ye ken. It wis a cannie thin thit ye did for yon wee burdie.'

And all Archie could do was to nod his head for he, too, had been thinking of the little dead kittiwake and his own life, and life's journey for all living things.

Countryside and Coast
by Tom Murray

COUNTRYSIDE: Selkirk

Ettrick River rush.

Dog's splishy splashy bath.

Our riverside couch.

COUNTRYSIDE and COAST

Memories swim

Catch in the coastal net.

River, sea, as one.

COAST: Eyemouth

Our boys' sea rush.

Fish suppers and sandy sun.

Runny ice cream faces.

Tweed
by Jane Pearn

This wandering trickle of mercury
      on the map, this liquid road,
path and traveller both,

      patient (has no lifetime), shapes
hills, gouges valleys, seeks to redefine
      its borders – recognises none of ours.

Left to itself unbounded would have
      no edge – spread molecule-thin,
would gauze the land with water.

Confined, asks relentless questions
    of its banks, tests
        for weakness,
    combs through grasses,
  eases soil
from roots, invisibly shifts
      mud-sludge, gravel-grains.

Defies the odds
    against it,
argues with rock
    and wins.
        Eventually.

In spate, rips at the
    restraint of channels, in
      impartial rage lifts trees,
        enters houses,
    exacts payment
for its long imprisonment.

Yearns toward the sea,
    tumbles in eagerness
  to bring perpetual gifts, silt and stone,
souvenirs of the journey it can't help making.

Sea honours the tribute, shifts and sighs,
exhales her gratitude in clouds which feed the giver.

You go for a walk with your mother
by Jane Pearn

We wind uphill, you with your long legs loping ahead. I pause often, catch my breath, apologise. You laugh at me, but kindly.

A peregrine's thin scream rips the sky, thrills our blood. There are quiet stars in the cropped grass: your shadow now out-lengthens mine but still I can teach you the names of flowers.

A levelling path, a sudden corner turned. Loch Skeen, a piece of mirror dropped into the cleft of hills. We marvel at its ice-pure water, speculate about rocks and time.

You are restless, eager to explore; but I perch on a tussock sprung from dense dark peat, listen to the water's lap and ripple, watch the circles widen from a rock's jut.

Glancing up to find you vanished, I feel the sickening swerve behind the ribs that mothers of lost children know. I stand abruptly and see you across the water waving, already more distant than I had supposed.

Mirror
by Jane Pearn

The Haining, Selkirk. I have been walking by the loch. The path is black mud, churned ankle deep, pocked with pools of yellow. At each step, my boots suck at the soft, rich earth, footfalls muted. I stop to lean on the wooden rail of a viewpoint. I watch the trees, still bare, mirror themselves. Their water-images – so clear, so silent – could be roots. I feel in my pocket for my notebook and a pen.

I stand quite still, noticing rough bark, smooth bud. On the other side of the loch, two figures appear. One wears a red coat, the other black, or maybe it is grey. They lean on a wooden rail. Their feet are hidden by a blurred fuzz of rushes, their faces indistinct. If they look across they will see a figure in blue, her feet hidden by a fuzz of blurred rushes. She is writing in a notebook. A mallard swims between us, leaves a silky vee that melts back into the soft water.

The figures, one in red, one in black (or perhaps it is grey) move away into the trees. I stay, watching the water, listening for words. A cloud drifts across the still surface, without disturbance.

I start to feel the chill and need to move. The path curves imperceptibly. Now there are new footprints in the dark soil – and here is the place where they stood. I look across the water. There is a figure in blue. She is writing in a notebook.

A mallard swims between us.

The Borders Countryside: A Snapshot of Places Seen
by Raghu Shukla

"A thing of beauty is a joy forever"
- John Keats

According to the Oxford Advanced Learner's Dictionary, countryside is the land outside towns and cities, with fields, woods and farms. The term is usually used when one is talking about the beauty or peacefulness of a country area. In writing this piece, I have taken the liberty of using this label in its widest sense.

Born and brought up in an Indian village, skirted by a river on either side, I am well aware of the splendour of the countryside. I moved to Melrose nearly a decade ago and haven't thought of living anywhere else. The Abbey, the Eildon Hills, the Tweed and nearby Abbotsford are unmistakable testimonies to this line of thinking.

Thankfully, the Scottish Borders has managed to retain its natural beauty in spite of its eventful past: three hundred years of Anglo-Scottish warfare. Thankfully, with the Union of the Crowns in 1603, the truce prevailed. Well, mostly.

In this short article, I have provided a snapshot of my countryside preferences:

Around my apartment: The woodland and the Eildon Hills

The allure of the countryside begins on my doorstep. The woodland begins only yards away from my apartment, providing year-round enjoyment. The spectacle during autumn months – the multi-coloured leaves in particular – proudly echoes New England's quintessential autumn landscape. Grey squirrels (alas, no native red ones) are frequent visitors and occasionally a deer has been spotted at the edge of the woodland. The winter months provide a different perspective to the area, bringing layers of ice to the trees' leafless branches. Dazzling is the word which easily springs to mind.

The Eildon Hills

The Hills are at their best in the winter months when topped with snow or covered with fog. These triple-peaked, heather-covered volcanic relics are like sentries above Melrose. They proudly dominate the landscape in this part of the Borders. The paths leading to the Hills are a walker's paradise for locals, visitors from other parts of Scotland, Northumberland, and for the European holidaymakers who descend on Melrose every autumn.

The Hills radiate grandeur as well as serenity; one receives a mysterious and spiritual impression from them – even more so in winter, when they are snow-capped or enveloped in fog and mist. I am lucky to be able to take in the scenery from the front entrance of Dingleton Apartments.

The Tweed

There is something special about the river Tweed. It has been called a 'graceful' river. I concur with this assessment wholeheartedly. In view of its meandering course, one meets up with it at various places in this part of the Borders. It must have been inspirational to Sir Walter Scott when he was writing all of his tomes (as we all know, the Tweed passes via Abbotsford House, the country house of Scott). My regular walks along its banks in Melrose are immensely pleasurable; talking to the fishermen and listening to the river's melodious roar as it flows along its rocky bed.

Fields, Fields and More Fields

The specific reason for my drives to Kelso from Melrose is this: to stare wistfully at the surfeit of fields dominating the landscape during the twelve-mile route. The arable fields are strongly reminiscent of my upbringing in rural north-east India.

The beauty of these periodic trips lies in watching the different stages of agricultural yields – mainly grains – from sowing to harvesting. The fields strewn with bales are all the more spectacular. Of course, the islands of tall trees, the ubiquitous Tweed and glimpses of the turrets adorning the magical Floors Castle on the outskirts of Kelso, also vie for my attention or anyone else's.

Paddocks

Horses are a common sight in the landscape of the Borders. In fact there are three paddocks within half a mile of my Melrose apartment. Why is this so? I wonder from time to time.

But first I should reveal my own interest in horses. I used to ride a pony and later a horse during my childhood in India; I used them to visit my relatives in nearby villages. Here in the Borders, horses seem to be a symbol of wide, open and non-industrialised countryside. Whatever, every year I watch with great interest the processions during the Common Ridings celebrations, which take place in various Border towns during the three summer months, June to August.

The Cheviot Hills

If I ever feel stressed, the effective treatment is to drive to Hawick via Selkirk on the A7. A few miles south of Selkirk, the peaceful, rolling hills of the Cheviots dominate the horizon and take the breath away. It's so soothing to both the eyes and the soul. Happily, the route I follow is not an exclusive one. That striking view can be enjoyed from a host of other places in the Borders. I have never been close to it but I understand that it forms part of the boundary between England and Scotland.

Let us now briefly consider the wider picture, well beyond a stroll in the countryside.

Apart from providing food for the body and soul – physical and mental benefit – the countryside also echoes the vision and efforts of previous generations of naturalists and conservationists from every strata of society and from all corners of the world: from Dunbar-born John Muir to the presidents of the United States of America. That's a lesson for us all. We should leave behind a better countryside than the one we found, benefiting both human beings and wildlife.

Happily, enjoyment of countryside scenery is not only derived from walks but encompasses other means such as cycling, driving, flying and a host of other sporting activities.

I end this piece with a reminder. We must respect the weather when we are out and about, irrespective of where we choose to go. This is because of its unpredictability, as well as the havoc, which is so often caused by its vagaries. We should, therefore, be "well equipped".

Finally, a personal experience sums up the above-mentioned predicament. A week before Christmas (2018) on a dry day, I was returning home. It was just getting dark. I suddenly found myself on all fours on the concrete footpath along the bushes. Luckily, I was about 200 yards from my flat. So why did I fall? Most likely it was due to my carelessness: I noticed that I had stepped on wet leaves and was wearing unsuitable walking shoes. (I confess, I was also mulling over no-deal Brexit.) The serious point I am making is that we should not blame the weather for our woes. The problems stem from the fact that we are badly dressed for the occasion.

Further Reading
1. The Borders *by F.R. Banks*
2. Border Country *by David Steel*
3. The Borders *by Alistair Moffat*
4. 25 Walks: The Scottish Borders *by Peter Jackson*
5. St. Cuthbert's Way: Melrose to Lindisfarne *by Ronald Turnbull*

Hold Up the Fish
by Keith Hall

Let's start up there, there on up!
Going down the river is better than going up!

You could also trip up.

Because at the end of the line the fish has to rise up.
It's all to play for with the weather on the up.
With three fish in the bag, 'keep your eyes shut'.

It's all down to luck.

With the wind blowing and the river flowing
The sun and then the rain the river is slowly rising up.

Holding on to the river oh…
We must go!
Hold up the fisher oh…

Let's have one more cast we're having a blast!
'Come on, let's go back to the car fast.'

Hurry!
Keep on up!
Pick your fly up!

'Now, let's pack up the fishing gear.'

On the best day of the year!
At last we weigh the fish up,
before we gut the fish up.

Back then I was a bit squeamish.

When we did go back on the same river
With my brother and my father.
On our favourite section of the river.

We always have a competition,
to see who has the best fish.
Whenever we catch a fish,
We hold up the fish.
Exciting for us fishers...
Bonnie eyed fish!

The Gorse in Bloom
by Pamela Gordon Hoad

Where did the birds go? No one could tell him and few of the villagers were interested in the puzzle. Some came in the spring and disappeared before the leaves began to fall. Old Oswin said they spent the winter at the bottom of the sea, far out beyond the stacks and scattered rocks, biding their time until they resurfaced and found ledges and crevices where they laid their eggs. Other birds came with the autumn winds, blown in perhaps from lands beyond the horizon, if there really were such places: skeins of geese flying inland to settle for a while on the loch behind the cliffs, where Grandpa had his cottage, and pretty crested creatures which stripped the berries from the trees and then took off to look for other feeding grounds. So Wilfred supposed and no one could say otherwise.

His mother didn't encourage day-dreaming, as she called it. What use was it to speculate about things that could not be known, mysteries which could never be solved? The fishermen, like his father, paid a bit more attention to the world around them. They could tell from the massing of the clouds and the bite of the wind if a storm was brewing and it would be hazardous to put out in the boats. They even noticed when the great white birds circled and then made for the rocky island in the distance where they nested, careful to avoid being caught out at sea in a tempest. Old Oswin, the boatbuilder, had a tale or two about foolhardy fellows who'd taken their coble out when the signs were unfavourable and come to grief on the reef within sight of the harbour.

Full of cautionary stories old Oswin was, exciting ones too, if a mite far-fetched sometimes. Like the one about raiders who'd come so long ago Oswin himself had been no older than Wilfred was now. Raiders in fancy long-boats with shields along the side, clutching axes and spears and firing the houses by the shore while the villagers fled in terror. If they could, the old man murmured. Wilfred wasn't sure he believed that story but Oswin claimed his elder sister had been carried off by these strangers and when the boy asked his mother about it she pursed her lips and prayed aloud that the raiders would never come again. Funny words, she used, like pillage, loot and rape. He understood from her expression that these weren't topics to be referred to lightly.

Ebba sometimes sat beside him, listening to old Oswin's stories; her eyes round like sparkling black stones on the shore and her rosy mouth falling open. She liked the tale of the seal-woman who wed an ordinary man, but one day slunk back into the sea, leaving him with a child who was half fish. She giggled at that. Ebba giggled a lot and Wilfred enjoyed the sound of her laughter, but he knew his mother mustn't overhear it too often. Ebba came to help with the cooking and mended their clothes, but she wasn't supposed to waste time enjoying herself. She wouldn't be helping them for much longer because when the moon had waxed and waned twice more she was to be hand-fasted with Malloch, one of the men who fished alongside Wilfred's father. That meant she would go to the new cabin Malloch was building above the beach and soon after that her belly would swell and she might die. That was what happened to girls.

This wasn't wisdom Wilfred had gleaned from old Oswin. His stories didn't deal with such things, but when the women gossiped they whispered about frightening occurrences, frightening but intriguing. Wilfred's mother didn't know he was listening to what they said or she'd have shushed her friends and stopped their chatter. Once, when he'd overheard them muttering about a baby born with twisted feet, he had dared to ask a question, but she slapped him and told him not to repeat such nonsense, it wasn't for boys' ears. That was puzzling but he learned his lesson and in future he pretended not to hear but played at his mother's feet, arranging shells in front of the doorstep and imagining they were strange boats sailing into the bay to loot and rape – whatever that meant.

He knew that it was true about women dying when their bellies swelled. That had happened to one of his aunts when she left a scraggy infant in his uncle's arms, but it had died, too, after a few days. His mother had nearly died the winter before last. She'd been ill for a long time after the baby was born dead, Wilfred's sister that would have been, and she told one of her closest friends that she wouldn't be able to have another. Wilfred didn't understand how she could know this but it was true she hadn't swollen up again.

Wilfred longed to be old enough to go to sea with his father and he loved clambering round the boat when it was beached after they'd brought in the crabs. He crawled under the plank bench, scrabbled in the seaweed tangled over the hull and tried to lift the heavy oars, but he wasn't strong enough for that yet. His father didn't grumble at him, not like his mother when he got in the way of her cooking pots or knocked over the kist of oatmeal. His father made a fuss of him and told him he was "a bonny wee fisherman". He liked that and he adored his father.

One day Ebba hadn't come to listen to Oswin's stories, up on the clifftop where they sometimes sat. Wilfred hadn't seen her at the house, helping his mother, and he wondered where she was. He asked Oswin if he knew but the old man made an odd whistling noise with his mouth and muttered something about her being ripe for plucking. It made her sound like a chicken or one of the sour fruits on the brambles. Oswin said she's been named in honour of a princess who'd lived years earlier, a princess who'd become a nun and founded a nunnery near their village, only her name may have been different, he wasn't sure. Wilfred wanted to hear more about princesses and nuns but Oswin didn't seem to know a lot – only that nuns didn't swell up and have babies. Princesses probably did, but this wasn't clear. Oswin went on swiftly to tell him a tale about monsters from the sea carrying off inquisitive small boys so Wilfred held his tongue. He understood Oswin was teasing him.

The next day Ebba came to help clean the house, but she didn't join Wilfred sitting with Oswin down by the little harbour. This was probably because his mother had been sharp with her when she appeared, calling her a lazy good-for-nothing who'd better look out she didn't lose Malloch if she couldn't care for him the way he deserved. Wilfred pondered what Malloch deserved because he thought the young man boring and he knew Oswin thought so too. All brawn and no brains, the old man said. Wilfred liked the rhythm of those words and found them funny.

He walked with Oswin up the slope of the cliffs, slowly because the old man didn't have the breath he once had, and they found a cluster of tiny white flowers in a hollow by a rock. Oswin said they were late coming into bloom and the winter storms would kill them. 'Not natural for them to open their buds so late. Now's the time for the seals to come to the bay, where the shelving beach is, to birth their pups before winter. Everything should be in its proper order.'

'The gorse behind the cliff, above Grandpa's cottage, blooms all year round.' Wilfred was pleased with himself for countering Oswin's assertion but the old man just rubbed his chin.

'There's a saying, Wilfred, that when the gorse isn't in bloom, kissing's not in fashion. Both go on all the time. Prickly stuff, gorse, too, and kissing's not much safer.'

Wilfred didn't like being kissed by relations and his mother's friends, some of whom slobbered, but he hadn't regarded the practice as unsafe. He was quite pleased to think he was right to wriggle aside when they bent their faces towards him, calling him "a sweet little fellow". What horrid damage could they do him? He didn't like to ask and Oswin had changed the subject.

When they returned to the village he saw his father's boat had landed so he ran down to the beach, but the men had gone and he made his way home, pursing his lips and trying to whistle like the older boys but without success. His father was already supping his bowl of potage and Wilfred was grumbled at by his mother for being late, but it was only a routine grumble and she did not refer to the various nasty fates that awaited badly-behaved children. He reckoned he had escaped lightly, but he was uncomfortable that they ate their meal in silence. Often his father was animated after coming back from fishing. He would tell them about the strength of the waves out at sea and how his boat had been nearly dragged into the dangerous current off the reefs as they came into harbour. Wilfred suspected someone was ill and his parents didn't want to talk about it in front of him. He was used to that and knew it would only provoke his mother's annoyance if he asked questions.

A few days later, Oswin was sneezing and didn't feel like climbing the cliff. He sat with Wilfred in the doorway of his cottage, showing him how to tie special knots which wouldn't slip, but he started to nod so the boy slid away to go up the slope on his own. It was a dreary, overcast morning but not too cold and he wondered whether the seals had come up to the beach yet. He'd like to be able to tell Oswin he'd seen them first and perhaps even spotted a pup. To get a clear view of the shelving shingle above the line of the tide, he scrambled down onto a ledge where there was a flat-topped rock, which made a good perch, and he crouched there peering down at the murky stones below.

They were simply the usual rocks, he decided, some covered in dried seaweed, some with lines of different colours along their sides, but all looking dull in the absence of sunlight. Then he noticed something different in one of the sandy crannies between ridges of rock where he liked to splash in the pools when the weather was warmer. There was a dark shape and it was heaving up and down in a strange manner. Could that be what happened when a pup was about to appear? Wilfred stretched out to get a better view and was intrigued to see something pale beneath the grey thing, which rose and fell, almost like a bare foot. Seal pups didn't have pink feet but Wilfred thought of Oswin's tales about sea monsters and the way they carried off fishermen and mermaids to their kingdom in the depths of the sea. Was this pounding object a sea monster? Was it devouring its prey? Wilfred couldn't hear any sound it was making because the swell of the sea was breaking steadily on the beach and there were gulls and the occasional oyster catcher calling as they passed overhead. Then the thing ceased to vibrate, flopping down on the pale creature beneath it, and Wilfred shivered. He was getting cold and he was afraid. Cautiously he raised himself up the incline and back onto the trodden path. Then he ran home as fast as he could.

His mother was frosty-faced and threatened him with a beating for splodging dirt on her newly swept floor. He crept into a corner and practised the knots Oswin had shown him, waiting for his father to return from fishing. But that was when his life changed forever because his father never came and never would.

It was next morning the men came to the door to tell his mother his father's body had been washed up on the beach below the headland, where the seals came. The women visited too to comfort her because the body had a deep wound in its chest and there was gore on the sand beneath it. Wilfred was told his father had gone fishing alone and he must have been swept out of his boat by a great wave, then driven onto the jagged rocks which stabbed him as effectively as a villain with a knife. It didn't make much sense because the sea hadn't been particularly rough that day but nothing was to be gained by arguing. Oswin took Wilfred to his cottage and told him stories to distract him from his misery but they were carefully chosen and didn't involve violence or sea monsters. He said Wilfred's father had been a fine man and the boy should never forget that. As if he would!

Life went on, as Wilfred learned it always did. Ebba and Malloch were hand-fasted sooner than he expected and, to his surprise, they moved away from the village, down the coast to the larger harbour he'd heard about but never seen. Ebba's belly had begun to swell, he thought, before they went and later he heard she'd produced a boy-child. She'd "pupped", one of the women said with a vulgar snigger. Wilfred didn't think it was right to speak of a woman as if she was a seal. He felt awkward and he didn't want to know what the women were gossiping about with their hands shielding their mouths.

He missed his father dreadfully, but Oswin did his best to entertain him and show him how to fashion figures and artefacts from wood with a little knife. Oswin became a regular visitor at their house and Wilfred noticed that his mother was comfortable with these visits. After a while she began to smile and even to cuddle Wilfred, which was unnerving but an improvement on her bad temper. Oswin also looked more contented than Wilfred remembered and perhaps he wasn't quite so old as the boy supposed. In the autumn of the following year, when the seals were expected on the beach once more, Oswin came to the house with a spray of yellow gorse in his hand and a few weeks later he took Wilfred's mother to the little chapel above the village and made her his bride.

All in all, grown-ups were weird, the boy concluded, but he'd realised it didn't always do to ponder deeply. Perhaps some mysteries should never be probed.

Newhaven
by Andrew James Paterson

Fish are gone, sun sets.

Empty market echoes still.

Bright yachts are lolling.

This haiku appeared on the Poetry Map of Scotland, No. 251

The Swimming Lesson
by Andrew James Paterson

One summer day, when I was a smaller child than I am now, I learned a little more about our family's peculiar and elusively unspoken history.

During the summer I always stayed with my paternal grandmother in her small house in the village. It was only yards from the harbour and the air smelled of tar from the drying nets and was full of the cries of gulls.

Because she was a widow and had been for many years, she kept the traditions. Grannie always wore black clothes. She was always in black, from the tightly-laced and highly-polished black brogues to the black jet brooch on her knitted black shawl.

My grandfather, grannie's man, had drowned off a fishing boat in the North Sea. His body had been washed up on the rocks outside the harbour. Just 50 yards from his home and 100 miles from where he'd disappeared over the side of the fishing yawl.

I was badgering grannie to give me permission to go to the baths with my pals. Grannie seldom let me leave the house without a few coppers being pressed into my hand. For the rest of it, I was allowed to roam the harbour free and clear with no questions asked and with no time limits. So her refusal was all the more surprising and resented.

I wanted to learn to swim. I was as persistent as only a single-minded child can be.

'But why not?' I asked for maybe the two-hundredth time.

So grannie told me why not.

'Sit yersel' doon, ma wee lamb,' said grannie, pushing me onto a stool facing her chair.

'Oor family' she said, 'and mony others aroond here, hiv aye worked at the fishing.

'The men folk worked on the boats and the women bided at hame and minded the siller.

'There's no been a man in the family, forbye the hale village, who could swim. No in the last twa hundret year. Nane of them went in the water at a', if it could be helped.

'The reason, ye ken, is that we're ower close tae the water. It's no the goin' in, it's the gettin' oot that's difficult.

'Lang afore ma time, yin o' the fisher lassies, yer ain kin, went wi' a silkie. A silkie is a craitur that's a seal in the water and a man on the shore, ma wee bairn.' She paused and her work-callused hand rubbed my hair.

'She soon left him, took a man over in Fife and lived a long time. But the silkie had left her wi' child, a wee girl it was.

'Onyways, the child had the silkie's blood. All the men-children from her side would be silkies. No help fur it. The call of the sea ayeways in the ear and the salt stirrin' in the bluid.

'An' you hae it an a'. If ye gaun in the sea, in the sea ye'll likely stay.'

I was a civilised child, intelligent and educated beyond my eleven years. I was smart enough not to believe her and rude enough to say so.

'Ah, weel then,' said grannie, 'bide there the noo.'

She rose from her chair and went over to the Scotch chest and pulled open a drawer at the top. A drawer so high I had not known it was there. She took out a brown paper parcel and came back to her seat. Grannie opened the parcel; her rough fingers pulled off the string and unfolded the thick seamed paper.

She set the opened parcel on my lap.

I looked at it and touched it. Inside the paper was a multi-folded piece of thin leathery stuff, with short, glossy, grey-black fur.

It smelled slightly musty and something else. It smelled of salt and wind from strange places, of the sea and far-off deeps. I shivered and goosepimples crawled on the skin of my back.

'What is it?' I whispered.

'It's yer granfaither's skin,' said grannie.

I didn't go to the baths with my pals. I've never learned to swim.

A Lad o' Pairts
by Rosalyn Anderson

Conflict is good but use of dialect should generally be avoided. This is the mantra of those instructing would-be writers and I have paid attention, except in my title, for reasons which I aim to clarify. Hopefully my decision would have been appreciated by Howard Purdie, the Lad of this piece. He was skilled in the use of controversy in his playwriting and poetry. He travelled extensively to expand his horizons and knowledge before the call of The Borders drew him back and his poetical imagination ran riot. In researching the many elements of his life, my journey has felt rather like an exploration of the tributaries of the River Tweed, which flows through Lower Tweeddale where he lies at rest. His life held many twists and turns, each one of such interest that removing even the tiniest rivulet felt wrong on so many levels.

Born in Dumfries, in 1938, a son of the manse, ("or more accurately son of Lucifer", he once dramatically stated), he was relatively sheltered throughout early years at Dumfries Academy.

Life changed dramatically with his father's call to Coldingham Priory. Re-located to the wild and windy Berwickshire coast, he spoke of his next schooling as "a lengthy and painful toughening-up process". Although in 1951 the Dickensian tawse still featured in Eyemouth Junior Secondary, his pupil counterparts from fishing and farming communities also contributed to this process. His learning was not just from academic studies. The hard life of the fishermen and families, their conflict between religion and daily temptation and the long-running impact on Eyemouth of its horrific disaster of 1881, was all stored for later use.

From school, he headed for Edinburgh possibly hoping for an easier life working as a librarian. Quickly frustrated, he felt his own calling: to explore the language of real people. His fondness for words was perhaps fuelled by the influence of Robert Burns. He gained great enjoyment unravelling the myriad dialects within the Scots language. He was aware of the many writers who had shaped Scotland's literary past and developed a particular affection for the poetical works of Hugh MacDiarmid. Hugh wrote extensively in Scots though in later life adopted English as his means of expression. I suspect Howard would have preferred the decision of an earlier literary man, John Leyden of Denholm. Advised during his travels to learn a little English, Leyden replied: "Learn English! No, never. It was trying to learn it that spoilt my

Scotch."

During Howard's journalistic career in London he was an enthusiastic member of The Player-Playwrights' Society, which enabled him to achieve, as he said, "a little success in the most difficult art form there is". The Society's Jubilee celebratory booklet[1] includes a reminder from Howard to only write about what you know and, most importantly, really care about. It was, therefore, initially quite surprising for me to read that he had produced a prize-winning play about the problems facing Sikh communities. It was then I discovered just how much I did not know about him. I cared enough to learn more. He travelled considerably across the Indian sub-continent and in so doing, developed a great love for India, Pakistan and Sri Lanka. He subsequently worked with Sikh communities in Edinburgh and Glasgow to gain even greater understanding of their culture and their challenges within Scotland. He entered his play in a Channel 4 competition and won. When his work did not progress to television as expected, he decided to use the £1000 prize to develop it into a well-received stage production in Edinburgh and Glasgow, featuring a wholly Indian cast - quite a trail-blazing decision for the early 80s which seemed so "very Howard".

Never wanting to be too predictable, Howard occasionally used pseudonyms for creative endeavours. This backfired memorably in 1984 when, as Jemina de Silva, he won first prize in the London Play Awards with a comedy set in Sri Lanka. Stepping up for his award, he was amused to hear Sir Richard Attenborough say, "Miss de Silva, I don't know whether to kiss you or shake your hand", passing him a cheque made out to Jemina (a Hebrew name meaning "listened to").

One of Howard's early highlights was the production of "A Fistful of East Wind" set in Edinburgh and staged at Edinburgh's Lyceum Theatre. This was in the late 70s, with a very young Gregor Fisher playing a riotous poet unpopular with the New Town elite. The play was, apparently, very well received, hopefully by an audience from both sides of the town!

Howard's father died in 1984 and I have no idea whether this influenced Howard's decision to head north and settle in Traquair near Innerleithen. He was firstly in a flat in Traquair House, the oldest inhabited house in Scotland, with its historic Bear Gates and own Bear Ale. Howard's creative imagination was certainly fired by his new environment, far from London, calmer than the windy coast of his youth and surrounded by his dear Scots language. In his poem, "The Bear

Aboon Traquair", there is a nod to the possible role of real ale in his conversation with a most uncommunicative bear (near Traquair!). An imaginatively illustrated[2] copy of the poem can be seen on the wall of The Traquair Arms.

Howard felt truly spoilt in this beautiful area, walking along Leithen Water and the Tweed as frequently as time, and latterly health, allowed. He loved his dogs and especially faithful Kitty, a rescue greyhound, and it seemed as if needy animals tracked him down. A failing lamb became his charge for almost a year. In keeping with Burns, who celebrated and mourned animals in poetry, Howard wrote a lament for Tibbie Clovenfoot. After this cloven attachment, which caused him not inconsiderable distress, Howard should have been wary of further unsolicited approaches from sick animals. However, he could not see a creature suffer nor perhaps miss an opportunity to surprise his neighbours! When Horace the Grey Heron arrived in his garden one winter, looking unkempt and hungry, he started to feed it regularly with chopped liver and haddock. This invoked correspondence from bird and animal charities, concerning Horace's sharp beak and the risk of over-reliance on Howard. Suffice to say, all was ignored and Horace returned for winter sustenance for several years. Although Horace the Heron has an alliterative attraction, Howard unsurprisingly had a literary explanation for the naming. The Greek philosopher and poet, he claimed, like a heron, stood about a lot in deep thought, admittedly without a sharp beak and not necessarily near water but simultaneously composing odes.

Howard soon began to explore the potential for drama, music and song in his new area, the Borders, with its rich history of literature, story-telling and traditional music. In proposing ideas, there were, inevitably, dissenters. Howard was not put off and creatively responded with a forthright "Polemic Satire of the Borders States". It included a most amusing and apposite map entitled "Border Country: Map for Europeans", featuring, amongst other points of interest, the Aye-Been Village, the Borders Ocean and a sign stating Europe's Ower There. This hopefully gives you a flavour of Howard's acerbic wit and the variety of opinions about that particular publication!

The long-running monthly performance events, entitled "Music, Verse and Stories", were initiated by Howard in Innerleithen and Yarrow and, over the years, many poets, singers and story-tellers participated, gaining confidence in a friendly setting. Everyone acknowledged their enjoyment by throwing coins into the Laird's Bunnet. This funded some interesting guests, persuaded by Howard's charm, to journey some distance for travel costs and perhaps supper. On my first visit, I recall my assumption that Howard owned a nearby estate. The bunnet's patina suggested considerable longevity, whilst Howard's own appearance never altered, his air of wisdom permeating his whole being, giving a lairdly demeanour!

One of Howard's more ambitious ventures was Supper Theatre, effectively re-creating Scott acappella dinners, a feature of 19th century Borders' literati. A top table of actors with scripted lines played Sir Walter Scott, James Hogg and John Wilson (better known by his pseudonym Christopher North) with Howard taking the Chair, as Henry Glassford Bell. The audience paid for their food, entertainment and, if they were lucky, claret, which Howard decreed essential to add atmosphere. One interesting occurrence involved a claret delivery intended for The Gordon Arms in Yarrow arriving in Jarrow!

Howard's comedic streak, coupled with his religious upbringing and ability to deliver a vocal performance in a range of tones and timbres, produced the character Reverend Jeremiah Aye-Been. The minister received excellent Edinburgh Fringe reviews and his name was, of course, inspired by the common Border phrase with the unsaid implication that things had best be left well alone.

It was certainly in community drama projects that Howard showed his true passion. A mix of professional people worked with a variety of community groupings, to tell a story. His final production achieved this on a grand scale, by realising his early idea of a play about Eyemouth. It wasn't quite his "Theatre of the Sea", envisaged in unrealistic dreams unfettered by finance and health and safety. There was no audience on the sea wall, there were no actors in real fishing boats and no retraining of Eyemouth seagulls, but it was truly memorable even though performed indoors and not always near the sea. "The Lament for the Little Boats" focused on the disaster of October 14, 1881, when one hundred and eighty-nine fishermen lost their lives. Ninety-three women were widowed and almost three hundred children left fatherless. Howard read the list of lost boats on the dartboard doors at The Ship Inn during a trip to the town and recorded the names. He then recited them endlessly and developed a lament with help from local traditional singers. He soon realised that it was not just a play but a multi-media musical performance which would best deliver this story. The attention to detail was remarkable, from torn-up strips of cloth on Fisher Lassie fingers (gutting herring was hazardous) to fascinating fishing industry footage from the National Archives of Scotland. Information from the historical division of the Meteorological Office explained the cause of the dramatic storm, officially classified as a European Cyclone. Stirring Methodist hymns sung by the Victorian choir reminded the audience of the religious fervour of the time, which sustained some fishermen in time of need. In stark contrast, the plaintive lamenting voices of the Fisher Lassies and their powerful acappella renditions of fishing songs emphasised the hardship endured in supporting the men. Dressed in working attire of the day, set against the Sunday best of the choir, the Lassies were encouraged to capitalise on the differences to heighten tensions. The audience felt the horror which would have been experienced as loved ones drowned so close to shore, and shared the women's fight to keep their fatherless children.

From inland Innerleithen in 2007, to Eyemouth and the Edinburgh Fringe, the piece of theatre which proved to be Howard's last, played to full houses and to phenomenal acclaim. It pulled no punches and did cause controversy in certain quarters. The disquiet concerned references to historical church tithe disputes linked to delays in harbour improvements, which could have ensured that more boats made safe haven that night. For the interested reader, the book "Black Friday", formerly published as "Children of the Sea" by Peter Aitchison, comprehensively details the disaster including tithe history, folklore and the resilience of the community. The tragedy is remembered in memorials and sculptures in Eyemouth and St Abbs and in a wonderful tapestry in Eyemouth Museum.

As one of the Lassies, I felt very privileged to play my part in such a moving and dramatic venture - the brainchild of a very talented man. I cannot claim that everything was plain-sailing but Howard "pressed home", like the little boats, regardless! To have pulled this off and taken it to so many venues was a great tribute to him and to everyone involved.

From his concern for the hard lives of fisher folk, I do feel a certain irony in Howard's concern for his starving heron, Horace, and the feeding of fish, hard-won no doubt by weather-weary fishermen!

Sadly in 2015/16, Howard received a terminal diagnosis. This, in addition to pre-existing conditions, increased his frailty. Rather than curbing his enthusiasm for life, and although almost house-bound, he published a selection of poems entitled "East, West, Hame's Best" using his beloved Scots words throughout. A wonderful image[2] graces the cover, as shown, of Howard with his devoted Kitty and the incorrigible Horace.

Even when he must have known life was slipping away, he dictated ideas for another play to his wonderful friend, the Innerleithen postie poet, Ted McKie[3], who gave him continuous hope and encouragement. Horace - the poet, not the heron! - coined the phrase "carpe diem" (seize the day). Howard, until the end of his life, certainly did that. Kitty pre-deceased Howard and died of natural causes. Horace presumably made the most of his latterly pampered life, as the average life span for the grey heron is only five years.

Ted and Howard shared a love of the Scots language, of nature and of the history of the area. Ted had written an amusing riposte to Howard's lament for Tibbie the lamb which delighted Howard. During his burial ceremony, which, at Howard's request, featured no minister and no religion, Ted read the poem, to much respectful amusement.

Howard's final act of creative thinking was out of the ordinary, whilst completely in character. Having no immediate family and with council rules for Traquair Cemetery encouraging purchase of two plots with literally, it seems, a two-for-one tariff, Howard specified the recipient of the spare plot, saying: "Tramps used to follow the byways of the Borders. There may not be many tramps left today - but if there is one who needs a grave, they can have it. I rather like the idea of a tramp being buried next to me".

(William) Howard Purdie died on June 20th, 2018, aged 80, leaving an amazing legacy and mixed bag of memories for very many people. He asked to be remembered as having had a jolly good time so here's to that and to the person who may lie next to him, in the beautiful Border countryside.

References/Acknowledgements
1. The Player-Playwrights' Jubilee 1947-1997 booklet, kindly donated by Peter Thompson of The Player-Playwrights' Society.
2. Joanna Powell, Howard's illustrator, for permission to reproduce her painting.
3. Ted McKie for provision of the photo of Horace and for contributing so much research material.

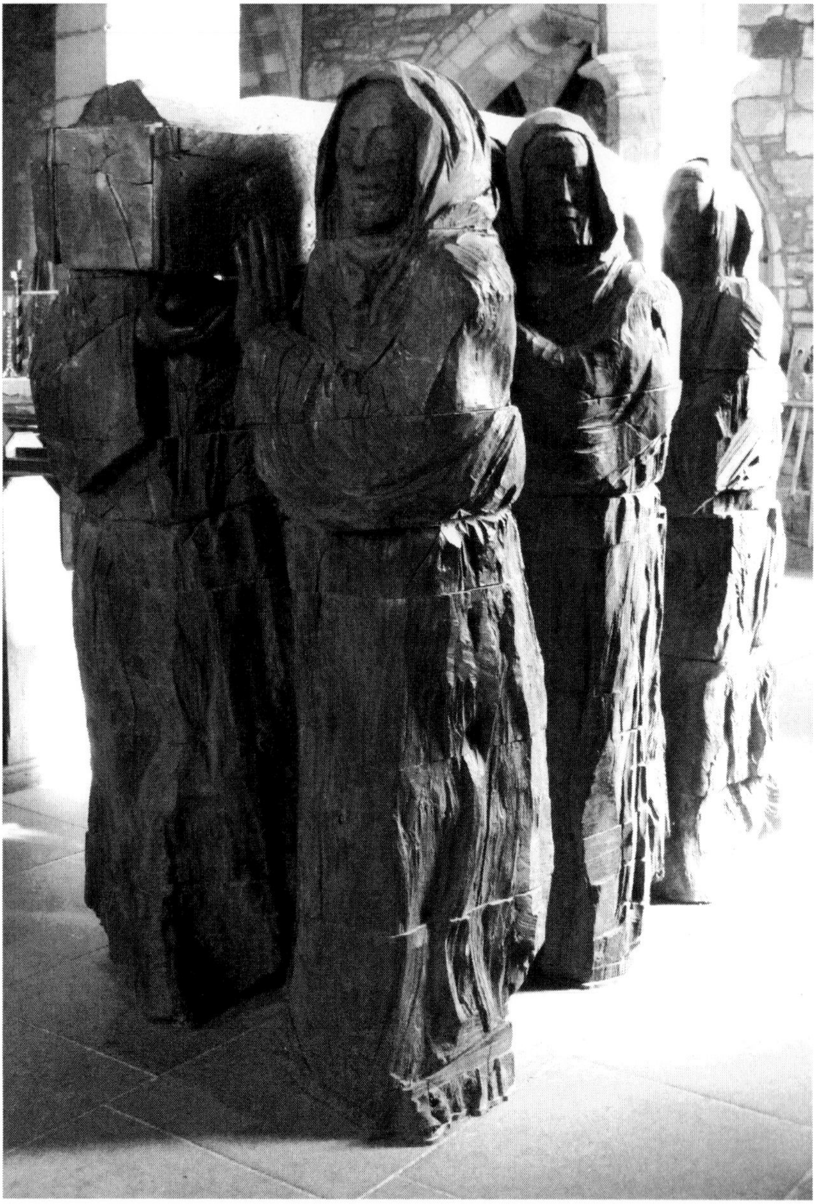

The Journey
by Laurna Robertson

In St Mary's the air
   is garden flowers and soft candle wax.
The sounds are paper.
   Rotas. Notes for visitors.

A calm presence
   in white light spilling from windows
stands at the heart of this afternoon;
   a knot of travellers.

Six monks carved in wood
   reach an arm across
to a brother's shoulder to steady
   a coffin with palms and fingers.

The hems of their robes swing.
   Wet sand and mud snatch at their heels.
On broken paths. Through rivers of rain.
   Past wild dogs' lairs.

In dust and damp sea mist
   relays of monks walking in step
carry, have carried tenderly,
   Cuthbert's perfect body here.

Fenwick Lawson's sculpture stands
in St Mary's Church in Lindisfarne

Ripples
by Sarah Johnston

There was something in the water. Coursing below the surface like a strong undercurrent or start of a swell; I'd never seen anything heave against the incoming tide like that before. It surged towards a pair of oblivious gulls drifting in the middle of the harbour. I took a deep draw on my cigarette and flicked the glowing end into the murky water. There was a loud shriek as the birds launched from the surface like torpedoes. They continued screeching as they circled overhead. Rolo, my chocolate Labrador, whimpered and took cover behind my legs. It was a Sunday afternoon in February so there was no one else around.

In summer, this area was crowded with annoying tourists, day-trippers and locals out for Giacopazzi's ice cream or chips. On dreich winter days, like today, only eager dog walkers ventured out.

Over on the opposite quay, near the water's edge, I noticed a large leathery stone like mass, perhaps eight feet long. Then it was swallowed by the rising North Sea tide.

'It would be a seal,' Jock said in the pub a half hour later.

Rolo stretched out in front of the log-burning stove, his chunky head heavy on the worn leather boots of Sandy McCollum, a retired fisherman and keen football supporter, who eagerly watched Hibernian versus Celtic on the television.

'Or a dolphin,' Sandy chipped in, his eyes fixed on the screen.

'Maybe it was a big salmon,' Jock suggested. 'Although wrong time of year.'

Back when the town was a vibrant fishing port, prawn creels and lobster pots stacked like tower blocks along the quay and boats berthed three-abreast the length of the docks. Jock and Sandy had crewed the *Mystic Star*, a large trawler. They knew the harbour better than anyone.

'So, not a crocodile then?' I uttered.

Jock snorted. Sandy nearly choked on his pint.

I'd seen crocodiles before at La Vanille Park in Mauritius. We'd visited there on our way back from Port Louis, where we'd collected the licence for our upcoming wedding. I enjoyed walking with the giant tortoises there, but Jackie was keen to see the crocodiles. At 4pm, we watched chicken carcasses hooked onto a chain and winched across a brown lake. The water was so calm and still one minute, but then a giant monster lunged out and tore the feathered meat from the chain before plummeting back below the surface. The ripples expanding towards the sandy shores of the lake the only hint to what had just happened.

'Ach! What had you been smoking, lad?' Sandy snorted, his attention now fully on me. My cheeks burned, and I scratched at my neck. Then I remembered an article in the local paper from a few months back.

'There was one found in Galashiels,' I offered.

'Yeah?' Jock's tone was sarcastic and dismissive.

'No. The laddie's right. I mind that story.' Sandy spoke up. 'Something about it being abandoned in an old pet shop or summat.'

'Aye, so maybe one escaped and headed down the river,' I added over-enthusiastically.

Jock shook his head.

'So are you trying to say that some old croc got into the Gala Water then joined the Tweed …. made its way out to the North Sea …. then came up the coast and into the harbour here?'

I wished for the floor to open and swallow me in one gulp. One day I might learn to keep my big mouth shut. He was right: it was preposterous to imagine I'd seen a crocodile.

'Well, I'm done.' Jock placed his empty glass on the bar. 'I'll let you know if I see a croc on my way home.' He winked, zipped up his jacket and chuckled as he walked out.

I tried to stave my humiliation and focus on the football. Hibs were winning. But the long, scaly form that I'd seen kept nipping at me like a nagging wife. Today was our second anniversary - well, it would have been had it lasted beyond the first two months. Irreconcilable differences, she'd called it. I called it being screwed over by a gold-digging slapper. Like the crocodile, she ripped apart my life then disappeared. She resurfaced months later, with some other gullible victim.

Suddenly the bar door swung open, slamming against a stool. Rolo jumped to his feet with his hackles raised. He barked as Jock charged back in coughing and spluttering. Jock fought to get his breath. He stood doubled over with both hands on his hips. I thought he was having a heart attack, but then he spoke.

'I saw it.' He grabbed and pulled Sandy from the chair. 'He's telling the bloody truth! Come and see for yourselves.'

Moments later, all three of us were looking out over the harbour. Rolo sat behind us, as if keeping well away from the water's edge.

Heavy grey clouds impaired what daylight there was, and the cold northern wind sent shivers down my back. I wished I'd grabbed my jacket on the way out.

'Over there.' Jock pointed to the opposite harbour wall. 'Below the cleat.'

It was difficult to make out clearly, lolling on the water line, but something long and dark kept vanishing then reappearing on the rolling tide.

'We need to call someone,' I said.

'Like who?' asked Jock.

'Coastguard, Police, Harbourmaster, Oh, I don't know,' I panted, shrugging my shoulders.

'We could always catch it ourselves,' Jock proposed.

'What! Now you've had too much to drink. There is no way I'm going anywhere near a croc,' Sandy spluttered.

'So, what do we do. We can't just leave it, what if it attacks a dog - or worse - a child?' Jock wrinkled his brow.

Police Scotland seemed to think it was some sort of hoax. Nevertheless, local officer Jim Watson was sent to investigate and found us back in the shelter of the pub.

Back outside again, we pointed over to where the croc had been seen, only now it was gone. The bobby's spotlight reflected yellow over the deep, dark dock. The tide was at its peak, as the water chewed on the harbour's edge. Jim, the policeman, prodded at the water with a long pole keeping at least a metre away from the harbour side.

'I've seen that David Attenborough on the telly and there's no way I'm going anywhere near the edge,' he said. 'Those crocs can leap some height.'

It was difficult to tell if he was being serious or taking the mick, but his search ended almost as soon as it began. Poor light and tidal currents made it too dangerous to do anymore, he explained. Of course, if I'd reported seeing a dead body then it would be different. A dubious crocodile, however, could wait another day.

I arrived at the harbour the next morning to find it buzzing with people. Crowds gathered, filming and taking photographs. Blue and white police tape cordoned off the area of the search. Police cars and Coastguard trucks defended the edge of the harbour from the press and eager onlookers, while two dinghies slowly crossed back and forth. Their spluttering outboard motors agitated the water. Onboard, men in bright yellow oilskins dragged poles and nets through layers of sludge. Quite a spectacle for our small town. News of the search swept across social media and local radio. I tried to keep my distance, but Jock spotted me and beckoned me across.

He was standing with a film crew and a reporter and he was grinning like the cat that got the cream; loving his twenty seconds of fame.

'This is the lad first spotted it.' He slid his arm over my shoulder like a proud parent.

'What did it feel like to come face to face with a killer croc?' The blonde female reporter asked thrusting the microphone towards my face.

'I....' I stuttered, startled how quickly my assumed sighting had grown into a full-size attack. Although in this town that sort of thing shouldn't surprise me. After Jackie left me, there were all sorts of stories growing like mushrooms and spreading like spores. Like she had won the lottery and was cruising the Caribbean, or she had run off to Portugal with her Spanish lover and the best one was that I murdered her and dumped her body at sea. How often I wished that to be true. Any of those would have been better than the truth, that she found me boring and unmotivated.

Even now, in my spotlight moment, I couldn't stand up for myself and explain what I'd seen. I muttered something incoherent and walked off, pushing my way through the growing crowds.

I tried to seek solace in the pub, but it was heaving with people and now it was the centre of search operations. The smell of coffee sailed around the room.

'Our own celebrity,' said Kevin, the landlord.

The coffee machine hissed and gurgled as he frothed some milk.

'I've not seen it this busy since last summer's herring queen.' He placed the mugs on the bar and took payment from a young reporter. 'Made more in the past hour than I have in the past two weeks. I knew buying this machine would pay off one day.' He winked at me, like I was in some way responsible for his good fortune. These people were in search of an assumed crocodile when all I'd really seen was a brown leathery mass and startled seagulls. It could have been anything.

Suddenly the door opened, and a red-faced police officer peaked around the door.

'They've found something,' he stated.

Everyone piled out the bar towards the quayside. I followed, but stayed at the rear of the bustling crowd. The two dinghies and search groups gathered together by the cleat where we first saw the creature. The low tidal water level now rested a couple of metres below the quayside and less than a metre above the thick layer of sludge, which lined the harbour basin.

A large truck with a winch was directed towards the edge. Everyone gawked as a twisted metal cable was lowered towards the water. One of the yellow clad men attached a metal hook to a familiar looking muddy mass in the water. As it began to reel in, the winch screamed as if its catch was putting up a weighty fight. Eventually a long brown form writhed and uncurled on the quayside. The commotion in the crowd became louder as the mass lay lifeless.

'What is it?' shouted an excited bystander.

I'd spent enough time around ships and the harbour to recognise hawser rope. The woven coil of heavy-duty rope, twelve inches in diameter and used for towing ships. My mouth went dry and I felt the blood gallop through my veins. I gulped in short rapid breaths. This humiliation felt worse than that of my cheating wife. Any moment the crowd would turn to laugh at me. The local fool again.

Before they noticed, I smuggled myself down the steps to the isolated beach. I knew they grasped it was rope when a tide of laughter spread along the crowded quayside. I fled towards the grey rock face and coves that enclosed the bay.

The crocodile story would taunt me for the rest of my days. Small crabs scuttled into crevices as I stepped over rockpools. Seaweed pods popped with each step.

I leant against a rocky outcrop and lit a cigarette. A zigzag line was scratched through the firm wet sand. It was accompanied by unusual footprints on either side. Something had been dragged from the sea. Soon the tide would rise again, and all would be washed away.

The Long View
by Anne Stormont

Breath-stealing, steep climb,
slippery scree and wild wind
threaten the balance.

High plateau, broad view
ancient granite mountains
frame a scope of possibilities.

Perspective changing,
infinity overarching, and
myself, regrounding.

Sea Eagle
by Anne Stormont

Cliff-soaring, loch-skimming,
Thermal-riding, high-gliding,
Mighty-winging, eye-spying,
Fell-swooping, fish-scooping,
Jaw-dropping, show-stopping,
White-tailed eagle.

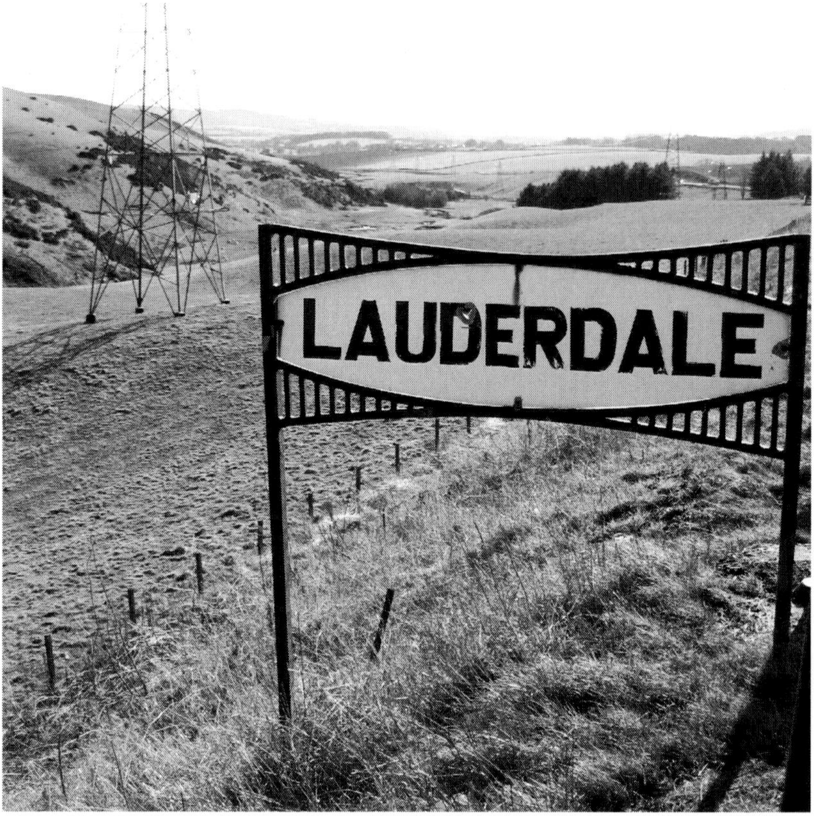
LAUDERDALE

Coming Home
by Vee Freir

Road twists as I breach the hill
wind turbines rise
like giants rooted, waving arms
to passing motorists

on to the double-laned carriageway
a final overtake before the long wind down
and that moment of coming over Soutra
when hills and valleys are exposed
cumulus clouds scattered in the sky
casting shadows across the landscape
and it seems as if there's no end
to the expanse of countryside ahead

another bend and
on my left-hand side
a board placed in a field
reads "Lauderdale"

I breathe deeply
an internal indicator
to the external sign
that says I'm almost home.

Troubled Waters
by Barbara Pollock

'It's a bridge,' Scott Milne, the owner of Milne's Mill said firmly. Dressed in a casual blue sweatshirt with the firm's yellow M&M logo, he exasperatedly pushed back a lock of fair hair that had fallen across his brow.

'No, a table between two people is a barrier,' Jason Swineborn, the firm's portly accountant, shouted back at him going red in the face. Taking off his suit jacket, he hung it on the back of his chair, and rolled up his shirt sleeves.

'Not necessarily. Think of a romantic dinner for two,' Scott replied evenly as he caught my eye.

'Utter rubbish,' countered Jason.

The rest of the firm's management staff watched in silence, with a mixture of horror and bemusement as Scott and Jason continued to argue with each other.

'A table can be a bridge between interviewer and interviewee,' I suggested calmly. 'It's time for a coffee break now,' I said bringing the first part of my training session on "Interview Techniques", to an uncomfortable stop.

As I helped myself to a much-needed coffee and piece of shortbread from the refreshments table, I overheard two of the women from accounts complain:

'Ever since Mr Milne Senior died and Scott had to hotfoot it back from Thailand to take over the helm, the pair of them have been locking horns like a pair of rutting stags. The mill's in enough trouble as it is without them at loggerheads.'

'Jason has never forgiven Scott for stealing his girlfriend and running off with her to the Far East. Pity she never came back. That would have been interesting.'

'Got a better offer so I hear,' the other woman confided.

I turned away. My stomach churned. I knew all about betrayal. The women scurried back to their seats when they saw Scott coming towards me.

'Jayne, I'm sorry about what just happened. Jason can be a bit hot tempered. My father's death has had huge financial implications for the business and he is trying to do his best.'

'Don't worry about it,' I replied smiling up at him, trying not to be distracted by his good looks and considerable charm.

I was glad when the day ended and I made my way back home. It was six months since I'd relocated from Newcastle to the Scottish Borders and set up my own business as a freelance trainer in business skills.

My mother had tried to talk me out of it, 'Jayne darling. I know things have been difficult for you after what happened, but moving to Scotland isn't the answer. You'll know no-one and setting up your own business is always risky.'

Mum was right, it had been a big step but a new start was exactly what I had needed so I didn't have to suffer people's sympathetic comments and uncomfortable looks. I had worked hard and picked sufficient up work to be able to manage financially. I loved the Borders' countryside with its ever-changing vistas and enjoyed long walks with my new companion, Bess, a three-year-old Border collie that I had got from the local rescue centre. I set off early each day before my appointments to take Bess for a walk, so that she could be left in the car until lunchtime.

That first training session at Milne's Mills can't have gone too badly because Scott Milne phoned me the next day and invited me for lunch in the mill shop café. He booked several more presentations, as well as inviting me out to dinner. We went out several more times, but, as much as I liked Scott, I wasn't ready to make a romantic commitment. I made the excuse that it wasn't professional to have a personal relationship with him while I was working for the firm.

As well as a downturn in the knitwear market Milne's faced a more insidious enemy. Rising water levels meant the river, once the life-blood of the knitwear industry, was in danger of flooding the ground floor of the mill. Even with the proposed flood protection scheme, the factory was in a precarious position. Scott and Jason were torn between waiting for the scheme to be completed at some future date, or abandoning the premises and building a new factory on higher ground, but as Jason kept saying: "the firm can't afford to invest in new equipment let alone a new building".

Over the next few months I felt the two men were using me as a go-between. The session I planned for them on negotiating techniques was even more fraught than the initial session, as each scenario I set up revealed the gulf between them.

'Look, Milne's has never been a pile 'em high, sell 'em cheap firm. We have always stood for quality. That's what our customers want and expect,' Scott said adamantly.

'But with this recession there are hardly any of the traditional customers left,' Jason replied, squirming uncomfortably in his chair. 'We should be looking for new markets. Em, we've been approached by a firm in China, who is willing to pay handsomely for the Milne brand.'

'What? Sell the name to some Chinese firm and have the market flooded with cheap Chinese imports - all with Milne's Mills blazed across the top? My father would turn in his grave,' Scott replied angrily, banging his fist on the table.

'Look guys this is only role play. No need to take it personally,' I assured them, worried things were getting out of hand.

'No. It is true,' confessed Jason turning to face Scott. 'We got an email last week. I just hadn't had the courage to tell you. I needed the right opportunity.' He pulled out a piece of folded paper from his jacket pocket and handed it to Scott. 'Mr Chang, the owner, is coming next Monday to look round the mill.'

'What? How dare you set up a meeting without consulting me?' roared Scott as he rose from his seat and towered over Jason, threateningly.

I thought the two of them were finally going to come to blows. I gently put my hand on Scott's arm to try to calm him down. I hastily set up a series of practice negotiating sessions with the two of them and Scott invited me to be part of the negotiating team. All sections of the mill busied themselves in anticipation of the three-day visit from the Chinese delegation.

'I'm pleased to meet you Ms Greene,' Mr Chang said as he shook my hand and gave a tiny bow.

'It's Jayne,' I replied tearing my eyes from his intense gaze as I returned his bow.

'You can call me Bo. It means "waves", in Chinese,' he added, smiling.

'Well, I hope you won't be making too many waves today,' I replied, returning his smile. In his mid-thirties, he was younger than I'd expected. He spoke perfect English so there wouldn't be a language barrier.

Bo Chang's delegation was well organised. I was impressed by their excellent presentation, complete with detailed business plans, flow charts and spreadsheets for alternative options. They had brought samples of the company's products. All made in high quality cashmere, they were certainly not cheap or shoddy.

After intense negotiations, rather than selling the brand name, they agree to form a partnership: Milne and Chang, with a new logo, M&C. Bo Chang agreed to pay the cost of installing new machinery in the existing premises, provided the flood defences were completed within six months. Jason pushed hard to get the flood barriers installed within the deadline. Scott and the in-house design team set to work on some new lines to complement six of the best-selling Milne products. The partnership with Chang's, however, caused unexpected ripples and I had a dilemma now that my sessions at the mill were coming to an end.

Five months later I stopped to take Bess for her morning walk. There had been a lot of rain over the previous week and the river was in full spate, but the sky looked clear. 'Plenty of time for a walk before it rains again,' I told Bess as I parked the car near an old packhorse bridge across a narrow section of river. I put her on her lead and headed for the bridge leading to a footpath through a lush meadow. Bess stopped partway across the bridge and excitedly wagged her tail. Jason, dressed in Lycra running shorts and top, waved as he ran towards us. He looked fit and healthy. I'd been surprised the first time I had seen him out jogging. Several stone heavier he'd worn a pair of ill-fitting jogging bottoms and a washed-out Spurs football top and was out of puff.

'The doctors told me I must lose weight or risk a coronary,' he had confided. Please don't tell Scott about my health problems.'

I kept my promise not to tell Scott, who never commented on Jason's weight loss. Since that first chance meeting, Jason often joined Bess and I on our walks and I'd even taken up jogging with him, with Bess running along beside us on her lead. It had come as a complete shock when Jason told me he had been offered a job in London and asked me to go with him.

Ever since I'd been left standing on the steps of the registry office while my boyfriend of four years ran off with my best friend, I'd been wary of being hurt. I was attracted to both Scott and Jason and was torn between the two of them. I had even gone as far as drawing a list of their strengths and weaknesses. I had told myself I was being absurd and to think from the heart not the head. Did I love both or perhaps neither of them? I'd even visualised the two of them in peril - which one would I save?

Bess barked. I turned round. A Land Rover with the new M&C logo came screeching to a halt. Scott jumped out of the car and came running towards the bridge.

He shouted, 'So the gossips are right. Jayne, how could you, of all people, deceive me? I trusted you.'

Jason ran towards us. Accusations flow thick and fast. I was in the middle of the bridge forming a barrier between them.

'Scott it's not what it looks like. I'm sure the two of you can deal with this like grown men.'

'Sure thing,' says Scott as he gently pushed me out of the way and launched himself at Jason.

A few drops of rain pattered on my face; a loud thunder clap could be heard in the distance. Then the rain pelted down in a heavy deluge. Bess barked frantically. The bridge shook beneath our feet. There was a rumble, and then a roar as a torrent of muddy water came thundering down the steam towards us.

'Run...' Jason shouted. As I dived towards the grassy bank at the other side of the bridge, Bess's lead slipped out of my grasp.

The level of the stream rose rapidly in a flurry of brown water, foaming with white-topped waves, bringing branches and fallen trees in its wake. Scott and Jason were still grappling with each other as the bridge was swept away; their shouts were drowned by the roar of the water as turbulent waves swallowed them up.

I screamed, 'Bess. Bess where are you?' I spotted her valiantly swimming towards the riverbank. She tried to clamber up the bank but her paws slipped and her lead caught on a rock. I ran towards her and scooped her up. Holding her close I dashed along the riverbank shouting in vain to Scott and Jason as they were carried down river. Their heads, close together, bobbed up and down like a mythical two-headed sea creature. Their arms and legs flailed frantically as they tried to swim through the angry water. I grabbed my mobile phone and hoped I could get a signal.

The two men were found several hundred metres downstream. The floodwater had washed down several fallen logs that dammed the stream and prevented them being swept further down river. Between them they sustained several cracked ribs, three broken limbs and numerous scratches and bruises. When I visited them in Borders General Hospital they were in adjacent beds, sniping at each other as I sat between them.

'It is a blessing the flood barriers had been completed ahead of schedule. They held back the water so the mill is safe,' I reassured them.

'Never mind the damn mill,' Jason interrupted. 'Jayne, please come with me to London. I'll be getting good money, not the pittance this skinflint pays, so we can afford to get a place near Hampstead Heath and we can take Bess for our daily jogs.'

'A pittance. You aren't worth the money I pay you. If it wasn't for Jayne and Mr Chang, the business would be in liquidation by now. Jayne, please stay here. The business needs you. I need you. I'll ask Mr Chang if we can take you on full time as our training officer,' Scott pleaded, trying to lift his bandaged arm to push the lock of hair from his bruised eyes. 'Ouch,' he groaned in pain, falling back on his pillows.

I finally snapped. 'I'm sick and tired being stuck in the middle of the pair of you, pulling me this way and that, making me feel like a feeble joke in a pound shop Christmas cracker. I've had a better offer.'

The door of the ward opened. Bo Chang entered carrying a huge bouquet of chrysanthemums in a dazzling array of purples, pinks and yellows. Both men looked towards him in expectation. Their faces dropped when Bo, bowed and presented me with the flowers. They sat stony-faced, both speechless for once.

'My dear Jayne. I am so glad that you have been able to find someone to look after Bess. Now that you have finally agreed to take up my offer to work for my firm, at our head office in Beijing for six months, there will be plenty of opportunities to travel and learn about the business … and to get to know each other better,' he added, as he smiled shyly.

I smiled up at Bo as I took the bouquet in my arms. 'I'm looking forward to it, but I will miss my dear Bess … and the beautiful Borders countryside, of course.'

Still Runs the Teviot
by Toni Parks

The insipid sun smiles on my valley-side dawn,
craggy outcrop reborn through burnt off mist.
Morning breaks over Fat Lips perch
its domain to survey, once more

And still runs the Teviot's north-easterly path
ever seeking out the sea

Contours and patches in pantone hues
cascade to the riverbank's side,
financial ruin lurks as a spiteful spate looms,
ruining crops, forfeiting livestock lives

But still runs the Teviot, where only the foolish
thwart history

Regiments of tall, slender, near-naked pines
play host to the woodpeckers' drills.
Patient buzzards camouflaged in coiffured treetops
calculate their prey's percentages

Still runs the Teviot, eroding its route
inexorably through my vale

A murder of crows cruises the six nine eight
on another all-day breakfast swoop,
a scavenging menu of road kill delights,
fresh badger and puree pheasant soup

Still runs the Teviot, paying witness to diners,
As it flows across my valley floor

Metal road so modern you cut me so deep and
leave nothing but pollution and detritus.
Your network links me to other villages and towns
where more of the same beckons

Oh, running Teviot sustain me and on,
for many more years to come

No leaping salmon now, on this ladder of success,
no water to slake the sheep's thirst,
only a bone-dry, stony bed, positive proof
man meddler meted out his own curse

Still the Teviot. It runs no more through me.

Welcome to the House of Fun
by Sandra Craig

'Good morning everybody! Are we all here, or is there anybody still to come in from the coach? No? Jolly good.

My name is David and I'm your guide today. Firstly, I would like to extend a warm welcome to this beautiful and historic house - home to many generations of the family, and still inhabited by them.

We keep them in the basement during the day, but we let them out to have the run of the place when we clock off after our shift. Just kidding!

I've been working here for several years now, and love meeting our visitors from all over the world. Oh, of course, you're just from Hull. Sorry, but your accents threw me for a moment. Oh well, this is bound to be rather different from your neck of the woods, eh!

Our tour will take approximately one hour, and I am happy to take your questions at any time, on the house, the family, their history, furniture, paintings and contents etc., so do please fire away.

This is the last tour of the day - and of the season actually - so we don't need to be in a particular hurry.

Oh, one thing I should mention now. Along our way you may possibly catch sight of an older gentleman in pyjamas, slippers and a faded plaid dressing gown. He is often to be seen scuttling along with a newspaper under his arm.

Worry not. This will be our Marquess. He doesn't usually get out of bed until lunchtime and has a habit of sneaking out of the private quarters to leg it to his favourite comfy sofa, which is located on this floor. It is his home after all.

Best to simply ignore him. He won't even notice you. No chance!

Moving on to the Drawing Room. This photograph behind me here was taken when he was much younger and had just recently inherited his title.

Yes. You are dead right, he doesn't look too pleased, does he? Wealth does not, of itself, bring happiness, at least not by the look on his face.

How did they make their fortune? Ah, a good, and frequently posed, question! All our visitors want to know the answer to this one.

How can I put it politely?

Way back in the 16th century, for men with ambition, and few scruples, the system in the south, and possibly across all of Scotland was to "get tight" - to use today's most apt expression - with the people in power i.e. the ones on a higher rung of the social ladder. If they were happy to have you around, they might then express their gratitude for your loyalty with a gift of land to farm, perhaps even the rights to some property.

If you've backed the right horse, as it were, your benefactor might then grow to trust you enough to give you the power to act as a steward, or agent, to keep the peace and "police" the locals, to damp down the worst of the blatant banditry by confiscating the stolen cattle etc. BINGO! You have now secured your future. And you can confidently continue your career in stock acquisition.

Yes. It does sound a bit like high-level thieving, doesn't it? Frankly, that is exactly what it was and it long remained a strong strand of the culture across this part of the country.

From then on, your loyalty to your mentors is your "golden ticket" to a rapid rise through the ranks - the top prize being a title. However, those could now become a rarity. These days I believe you have to inherit one from a dead dad, as no new ones are being created.

Anyway, here we are in the Day Room.

Nearly forgot to say, if you see a guy in his thirties, who looks like a handyman, pass by carrying a ladder and tools, and is a dead ringer for the Marquess, please try not to stare. Actually, we're not too sure about him either. Yes, it rather gloomy in here. Embarrassing to have to say that the housekeeper is only permitted to order 6-watt candle bulbs.

Anyway, moving on to the Library and the formal Dining Room.

As you will see from the information boards in here, the majority, if not all, of the furniture, ceramics, etc. on display arrived here courtesy of what one might call a "fortunate marriage".

Seems like royal patronage and local "mafia-type" activities were insufficient to fund the lavish lifestyles of the Marquesses, Dukes, Earls and Viscounts of the United Kingdom.

By the 19th century many of them were flat broke at best, at worst deeply in debt, and facing massive challenges with the upkeep of their crumbling country homes and town houses.

Co-incidentally, and happily for many of our indigent gentlefolk, the wealthy entrepreneurs of that era in the United States - who were much mocked, by the "Gentry" of the U.K. for their nouveau riche lifestyle - just happened to produce a raft of beautiful daughters. These eligible young ladies were, for the most part, happy to acquire status and titles on this side of the pond in exchange for multi-million dollar dowries.

Sadly, despite an intense and expensive wife-hunting trip to New York, our then incumbent, the Marquess's granddaddy, failed to attract the attention of a single one of that group of eligible girls. The results speak for themselves.

Our Marquess's dad did, however, manage to snag the younger daughter of a wealthy landowner a few miles from here. Her dowry was happily sufficient to include some very rare knick-knacks to brighten up the place, plus a wad of cash sufficient to hold the dry rot and rising damp at bay.

Anyway, enough of this blethering. We are now in the Kitchen and nearing the last of the exhibits.

I hope you have enjoyed your tour. Please don't forget to sign the visitors' book, and leave some nice comments on your experience before you leave.

I shall follow you out.

This is my last day here. The management probably don't know it yet. I've got a new job so I left my letter of resignation at the front reception desk this morning.

I'm right behind you, so please hold the door. I'll race you to the car park!'

Unleashed
by Hayley M Emberey

"It is getting a bit cramped in here. It has taken longer than usual, this journey. We must be going somewhere new and exciting. I do hope we will arrive soon. There might be loads of squirrels and rabbits to chase, some digging and burrowing."

The electric window shuddered as it slowly descended out of sight. As the cool, fresh air wafted in from the outside, the smell of salt touched Rufus's quivering and sensitive snout. A faint cawing could be heard and there was finally a sense of anticipation as the feeling of near-arrival tingled within his heart.

The car began to purr rather than hum as it reversed into a space and came to a halt. The wonderful creaking sound of putting on the hand brake resonated throughout the car. "Is it time to get out now?" Rufus thought.

As the hatchback door rose, Rufus gazed on to the new vista. "The rock, over there. Yes, it's one of my favourite haunts. It seems to have grown since I was last here, but it is still too far away to swim to. What's this? A piece of rope?" Rufus sniffed it curiously, with a pent-up passion. It had an unusual scent and, as his jaws surrounded whatever it was, the taste of salt rocketed to the back of his throat. Ratting it from side to side vigorously, just in case it was still alive, he spat it out onto the sandy floor. Now digging, both his front clawed paws frantically commenced a journey into the unknown, followed closely by his muzzle about to receive a gritty makeover. He quickly glanced backwards to see if he could spot the familiar silhouette in the distance known as his 'master'. He did and, with that comfort in mind, plunged into the waves.

Rufus's first thought on entry: "Just as well I have my permanent fur coat, for this feels somewhat chilly around my ears." He bounded further into the giant bath, popping white, frothy bubbles with his jaws. "Doesn't taste like the water they give me at home, but as if I care. This is heaven. I just have to breathe, paddle and am free!" A few more wavering motions of the water massaged the floating four-legged then that familiar whistle demanding his return resounded and penetrated the natural lapping noise of the waves, an unsubtle hint he was required to head back to the sandy shore. "Sorry, not yet, master. This is much too much like good fun to come back and see you yet, especially after being cooped up in that boot space for so long." Rufus looked around, at first, towards the end of his snout. The ripples of water were cruising in from all directions, illuminated intermittently by the reflection of the sun's rays. The flickering of light reminded him of the lights hanging in the window at home for a few days once a year.

Quite far out at sea now, his paws were truly in synchronised motion with the flapping movement of the waves, then the screeching whistle from his master, a little bit more intense this time, penetrated his soft, wet ears. The rock seemed much clearer now and had grown even more. The vast black lump against the horizon seemed to beckon him to come closer to it. Vague movements of tiny puffins flitting about in the faint crevices became visible as he approached. Would make a wonderful basis for a children's story full of imaginative adventure. Robert Louis Stevenson obviously thought so. The vastness of the horizon before him exuded a sense of freedom, infinity and wonder. Another screech, he guessed that's enough hints for it now to be time to turn back towards the shore.

Back on land, Rufus shook his sodden coat and, sniffing the air, bounded over towards a rug void of company, around which there was the delicious scent of hamburgers. On his approach, he sensed a shadow towering behind him. This time master was shouting. It really might be time to head back now. Rufus was scooped up, carried to the car and placed gently into the boot. Feeling soulfully alive and invigorated, the cramped space seemed less inhibiting than before, rather a nest of comfort in which to rest. If that was all his playtime was going to be today, Rufus decided to close his eyelids with contentment. Once the humming sound resumed, the bedraggled canine drifted away into a peaceful oblivion.

However, not long after, the distant, creaking sound of the hand brake startled the somewhat floppy and drowsy soul. He didn't recognise this new place as he jumped up to peer out of the hatchback boot window. As the door opened, he felt a spurt of emphatic power to leap out and be unleashed into the wilderness beyond. Manoeuvring a wooden gate, there lay a vastness of moorland of coarse bushes and a maze of wonder amidst thick, dried, straw strips, taller than the usual soft, moist, green blades to which he had become accustomed. "I'm going to run and roam and leap and be carried into this wild abyss, which knows no bounds," he thought. Galloping effortlessly, his heart pounded as the distraction of new smells of rodents and others of his own kind, pulled him here, there, and anywhere and everywhere across this plain of exquisite goldness. The precious terrain encased by a mountainous horizon, riddled with trees and scrubs and bushes, veered upwards towards a pinnacle, luring him towards it. The ascending silhouette of his adoring master let out another cry to summon the reckless meanderings of the frenzied Rufus to rather follow a flatter path carved by many a trodden foot, towards the top.

"Charge!" A temporary feeling of medieval thirst for battle, Rufus rocketed forth and stopped in the middle of seven mysterious looking objects, all with different carved faces. Their stony eyes were fixated on the new arrival, all holding different expressions, some more menacing than others. They didn't seem to move. They were completely still. They did and said nothing. As with most things, Rufus's attention span was short-lived and the only way now was down. Frantic digging followed, unearthing an abundance of bones. Another heavenly experience today, Rufus couldn't believe his luck. "Where did all these bones come from?" he thought. There was the screech again from his master's whistle, but as Rufus tried to move, he realised he was stuck. There was no room to get out. All was black, damp, muddy. He stopped panting for a moment and observed the space in which he found himself, feeling a presence of being surrounded by hundreds of years of history, a special place of ancient Earth. A sense of wonder befell him, then the faint sound of the whistle again brought him back to the present. There was nothing he could do though, apart from await the arrival of his master. He knew he wouldn't starve for as long as he was stuck down there. With a lick of his lips, Rufus started cracking through the bones. They were bigger than those he was used to.

Rufus's master approached the scene with hesitation and saw the hole down which his furry friend had fallen. The scrunching noise of eating bones echoed well beyond the seven stone plinths which had weathered centuries of both elemental and human contact. As Rufus looked upwards, fragments of mud cascaded into his sweet, loving eyes and, with a shake of his head and a sneeze, the caring hand of master was truly welcomed as it grabbed him by the scruff of his neck and pulled him into the fresh air. The sunlight was now beginning to dwindle. It was time to head back to the car. Rufus appeared to be decidedly untroubled by what had just happened to him.

One last sunset stop before home to the luxuries of his fur-lined basket heated by the tumble dryer, the car slowly came to rest. This new view of the countryside held a different feel to the previous location. Rufus looked out over a massive, landscaped carpet of yellow rapeseed. Weary from the day's adventures, he just sat and gazed through glazed eyes at what was once a battlefield. His master did the same stopping to think for a moment about all the years of slaughter of man slaying man in battles for land, country, king, queen or honour, which had taken place right here in front of them both. Who would have thought such bloodshed could have once prevailed on this now yellow haven? Content with their day out, Rufus coiled up like a white corn snake, already dreaming of his next adventure, sniffing new smells, chasing, digging and discovering. His master started the engine, transfixed by the beauty before him and sighed with gratification for the simple pleasure of being at one with the boundless and natural magnificence of the Scottish coastline and countryside.

Contributors

Rosalyn Anderson - After a pharmaceutical career, which included writing for academic publications, I am now enjoying learning more about creative writing in the hope of a future novel! A reminiscence and short story featured in two earlier BWF Anthologies, and I am in the process of writing my second companion piece for Berwick's Wilson's Tale Project.

Iona Carroll - I've lived in the Borders for thirty-four years; past secretary of the BWF for nine years; wrote, developed and taught a twelve week short story course; founded the Kelso Writers in 2012; joint editor of the *Eildon Tree*; member of the Society of Authors; written three novels; my collection of short stories to be published in 2019. www.ionacarroll.com

Sandra Craig - I have been drawn for some time to the theme of "Things I'd love to say, but daren't". The Borders is rich in castles and "stately homes" and it struck me that the personal histories of their inhabitants held potential for rumour and local gossip.

Hayley M Emberey has travelled to over 25 countries, lived in five and speaks three languages. Her mother's family are Scottish, her father's family are English and Scotland is her latest home; seen as a haven to enhance her new career, after years in International marketing and Deep Cellular Healing, in writing for children, adult fiction and self-help books. She particularly enjoys personifying her work where the imagination is stretched and limitless.

Vee Freir is an almost retired Clinical Psychologist who took up writing after moving to the Borders in 2008. She has written non-fiction books, poems, short stories and a play. Her latest book "Learn To Stress Less: 50 Simple and Effective Tips for a Stress-Free Life" can be found on Amazon.

Pamela Gordon Hoad had a career in public service and took up writing historical fiction in retirement. In addition to short stories, she has published four thrillers set in the Fifteenth Century featuring Harry Somers, physician and investigator. A fifth book in the series is due out in 2019.

Keith Hall is a motor mechanic from Duns, Scottish Borders. He first took up writing romantic poetry after meeting his wife Roz. His passion and interest in poetry grew with a desire to write beautifully worded poems that have a little twist. He enjoys writing poems that depict events touching his life, such as feelings for his wife, getting married, his father's wedding, the birth of his daughter Sasha, his hobby of archery, catching fish down the river Whiteadder, and volunteering with Northumberland Scouts.

Anita John is a published poet, fiction writer, playwright & Writer in Residence for RSPB Scotland Loch Leven. She writes drama with Playwrights' Studio Scotland, with work performed at Talkfest in the Borders 2018 & Borders Pub Theatre 2019. Her short play, "First Steps," will tour with Odd Productions Theatre, autumn 2019.
www.anitajohn.co.uk

Sarah Johnston is studying towards a BA in Creative Writing with the Open College of the Arts. "Ripples" was inspired by news articles relating to sightings of a crocodile on the Thames, and also the discovery of an alligator abandoned in a local building after a pet shop had closed down.

Robert Leach is a former chair of Borders Writers Forum. He has been working at the craft of poetry for nearly fifty years, and has published five collections as well as pamphlets and chapbooks. He is also a theatre practitioner and historian, who has worked in USA and Russia, and published many theatre books. The latest is a two-volume *History of British Theatre and Performance.*

Tom Murray is a playwright, poet and fiction writer living in the Scottish Borders. His recent plays include: *Lady Grinning Soul*, Short Attention Span Theatre Company, 2019. *What Lies Beneath*, Firebrand Theatre Company as part of Playwright Studio Scotland Talkfest in the Scottish Borders, 2018.

Toni Parks - my usual style of writing is Borders noir, so this poem is somewhat of a departure, although very pertinent with the Climate Change demonstrations taking place at present. I've now self published the *Gemini Borders Trilogy* plus *Winner Takes All?*, a stand-alone novel, and still find time to be BWF secretary, for my sins.

Andrew James Paterson When very small, I read everything; papers, labels, magazines, comics, books, more books, even more books. Transporting me to different worlds; Outer Space with Dan Dare, a steamship to Kilba, Conrad of the Red Town, adventure with Alan Breck. I wanted to create my own worlds. I still do.

Jane Pearn lives in Selkirk. She writes mostly poetry and short stories, and has two published poetry collections. She was longlisted in the 2018 National Poetry Competition, and is one of the winners in the 2019 Guernsey International "Poems on the Move" Competition.

Barbara Pollock In the late 1990s I attended workshops run by Tom Bryan, Borders Writer in Residence. I have had poetry and short stories published in anthologies. I am currently working on a novel for young adults as well as a family saga. I am inspired by the Borders countryside.

Laurna Robertson was selected by the Scottish Poetry Library to be one of five poets to read at the Abbotsford Showcase in 2013. Four poetry pamphlets have been published, including *The Ranselman's Tale* and *Praise Song*.

Raghu Shukla - an Indian village boy turned NHS hospital doctor, turned writer, is Senior Editor of an internationally contributed book on elderly care. His recently published memoir, which consists of 36 stories, is a blend of memoirs, medical and global-travel anecdotes, commentaries, essays and serendipitous moments. Raghu lives in Melrose, Scottish Borders.

Margaret Skea is passionate about authenticity in historical fiction. Her Scottish trilogy - *Turn of the Tide / A House Divided / By Sword and Storm* has received various awards including Beryl Bainbridge Best First Time Novelist Award 2014, Harper Collins Historical Fiction Winner, and Longlist HNS Novel Award 2016. *Katharina: Deliverance,* set in 16th c Saxony, was Runner-up in the International HNS Novel Award 2018.

Anne Stormont writes contemporary fiction where the main characters are older but not necessarily wiser. She hopes her stories will entertain, but she also hopes they will move, challenge and inspire. She has published three novels so far – *Change of Life*, was her first. *Displacement* and its sequel *Settlement* followed.
www.anne-stormont.com

Aims

- To promote interest and raise the profile of contemporary local writers
- To provide a focus for writing-related events in the Scottish Borders
- To provide networking opportunities
- To support professional development through talks, regular readings and workshops
- To offer fellow writers a friendly and supportive environment

Borders Writers' Forum meets monthly between September – June.

Further details, including a programme of events, available on: www.borderswritersforum.org.uk

"A mile of the beautiful turn of Tweed above Gala-foot"